"Ready," Henry whispered.

The door opened. Two of them came in single file and then spread out, one covering with his machine pistol, the other advancing to get behind them.

Carter waited until the advancing man was just in front of Henry, then he grazed Henry's back with the Beretta's short barrel.

Henry dropped like a felled tree and rolled as the Beretta began to chatter. Neither of the men had time to blink before they met their Maker . . .

NICK CARTER IS IT!

"Nick Carter out-Bonds James Bond."
—*Buffalo Evening News*

"Nick Carter is America's #1 espionage agent."
—*Variety*

"Nick Carter is razor-sharp suspense."
—*King Features*

"Nick Carter is extraordinarily big."
—*Bestsellers*

"Nick Carter has attracted an army of addicted readers . . . the books are fast, have plenty of action and just the right degree of sex . . . Nick Carter is the American James Bond, suave, sophisticated, a killer with both the ladies and the enemy."
—*The New York Times*

FROM THE NICK CARTER KILLMASTER SERIES

NICK CARTER

KILLMASTER

Circle of Scorpions

CHARTER BOOKS, NEW YORK

CIRCLE OF SCORPIONS

A Charter Book/published by arrangement with
The Condé Nast Publications, Inc.

PRINTING HISTORY
Charter Original/January 1985

ISBN: 0-441-10561-0

Charter Books are published by The Berkley Publishing Group,
200 Madison Avenue, New York, New York 10016.
PRINTED IN THE UNITED STATES OF AMERICA

*Dedicated to the men of the
Secret Services of the United
States of America*

ONE

It was exactly five-thirty when Nick Carter walked into the Oak Room of Manhattan's Plaza Hotel.

His date was for five o'clock, but she was still at the bar, waiting, an empty stool on either side of her.

She wore a green dress that had been cut from just enough material to cover the full curves of her body. As he approached, Carter noticed that her fiery red hair had been brushed into a theatrical kind of upsweep.

He smiled. The coiffure had been his suggestion.

Talon-tipped fingers were wrapped around a Manhattan.

"Hi." He brushed his lips across her cheek and then did the same to the back of her hand.

"Nick, I was beginning to wonder."

"Sorry I'm late. You know us tycoons."

Carter settled himself on the stool beside her as the bartender appeared in front of him with a wide grin on his face.

"The usual, sir?"

"Yeah," Carter said with a nod, and ten seconds later he was toasting the voluptuous redhead with a Chivas, neat except for a single cube.

"To us, Naomi."

"To another wonderful evening." She turned to him and smiled. Her generous mouth had a much too generous coat of brilliant lipstick. "Do you realize that it's been two whole weeks since we met, right here?"

"They've flown by," he replied in a husky whisper. "But more important than the past is the future . . . tonight."

"We'll see," she purred, lashes fluttering.

Yeah, Carter thought, *I can't wait much longer, and neither can David Hawk and AXE!*

Just that morning, the head of America's supersecret service had called the Killmaster back to Washington for a briefing.

"How much longer, N3?"

"I think—I *hope*—tonight's the night. Is Garrett ready?"

"Ready and waiting. He's been cooling his heels in New York for a week."

Carter had felt a wave of heat pass over his eyes. He had been taking Naomi Bartinelli out every night for the past two weeks.

Object: Seduction, to put himself and Al Garrett—AXE's resident electronics and computer genius—inside her apartment.

"I'm doing my best, sir. The woman likes to play hard-to-get."

Hawk had smiled. "According to your file, Nick, it usually doesn't take more than three evenings, four at the most."

Carter allowed his lips to form a smile. "Not every woman is in such a tricky business, sir. I've got to get her confidence—make her think that it's only her many charms that I'm after."

Now, looking at those charms encased in the skintight, silky dress, Carter emitted a low chuckle.

"What's so funny?"

"Just thinking how lovely and . . . desirable you look," he replied casually, warmly. "Ready for another drink?"

She upended the glass between her crimson lips. "Now I am."

Carter crooked a finger and the bartender was back, still grinning.

"Two more," Carter said.

They both fell silent as they watched the bartender scurry to mix the drinks. When he returned, their legs touched as they reached for them.

The electricity was immediate.

"What shall it be, Naomi? Dinner? Or should we just skip to the dessert?"

"Let's have dinner first." She smiled. There was a slight space between her incisors that marred an otherwise beautiful set of teeth. "I'm starved."

"So am I," he grinned, "but not for dinner."

"I told you, Nick," she said, her soft brown eyes sparkling from the drinks. "I like to be seduced. And seduction starts with dinner."

"Okay. Here?"

"How about someplace more romantic?"

"How about a little French place on the East Side? The food's great, the waiters do everything but shine your shoes, and the candlelight is so romantic you can't see who you're eating with unless you smile."

She glanced down at the dress. "Do you think I'm dressed well enough?"

"You look nice enough to go anyplace," he replied, waiting for a bolt of lightning to come through the ceiling for telling such a lie.

She wet her lips with the tip of her tongue. "Well, if you say so."

Carter sipped his second drink slowly, watching her. He tried not to let his gaze linger too long at her neckline, where an interesting battle of containment ensued every time she breathed in and lifted the glass to her lips at the same time.

He decided it to be a true test of his imagination to picture what she would look like if she were sitting there with her breasts completely liberated.

She finished her drink and touched his arm. "I'm ready to go anytime you are."

The restaurant was small, cozy, and as dim as Carter had remembered. It was owned by a Swede with an Italian wife, but they did have a French chef.

Nothing had changed since the last time Carter had dined there except the prices. They had tripled.

There were the same red velvet drapes covering the walls, the same copies of paintings from the Louvre in ornate gold frames, and the same omnipresent waiters.

Even before Carter's eyes could become accustomed to the subdued lighting, Naomi Bartinelli's presence stood out in the room as though a spotlight were being played on her. As the maître d' seated them opposite one another at one of the more secluded and intimate tables, he could see the woman as one would see a torch on a dark night. Her flaming red hair piled high on the top of her head was like a beacon, and the bright green dress against her white skin stood out in contrast with the basic red decor of the room.

"Would you care to order drinks, sir?" the man asked in a hushed voice that was in keeping with the general tone of the room.

Carter ordered, and when the drinks came he made an elaborate production of ordering dinner in fluent French.

Naomi Bartinelli was impressed. She was supposed to be.

"I didn't know you spoke French."

"Ah, my dear, there are many things I do that you do not know about. I have a lot of business in France, as well as in several other countries."

She sighed and sipped her drink. "I contact people in France, Germany, and Spain all the time, but I never get to go there."

"Oh? Just what kind of business are you in? You've never mentioned it."

She shrugged. "I play with computers. I . . . well, let's just say I relay things."

"Is your office here in the city?"

She nodded. "I work out of my apartment. It's more convenient, and . . ."

"And . . . ?"

"Nothing," she said, again shrugging her shoulders as a cloud passed across her eyes.

Carter didn't push it. He knew exactly what she did, who she did it for, and why she worked out of her apartment; it was more private.

And privacy, for both Naomi and her clients, was very important.

Her clients included gunrunners and smugglers, and underworld lawyers who wanted to stash or launder money abroad. She handled contracts for anything from a hit to a hijack abroad, or something simple like a message between shady friends who didn't want to use conventional—and tapable—means of communication.

For instance, if a terrorist group wanted to purchase a few hundred rifles, they would look up a broker. The broker would put the word out via Naomi's computer to the world's arms thieves. An available list would come back, and she would relay it.

If a deal were arranged, Naomi could also set up the buy and the place of delivery, and, by using certain codes, insure that the two parties could make the exchange in safety.

It was a neat little operation, requiring a very bright brain in computer systems and a knowledge of worldwide crime to set up.

For all of her lack of taste and class, Naomi Bartinelli did have such a brain. It was only after weeks of probing that AXE had found her Achilles' heel.

She worked very hard. Trusting no one, she usually had to stay in her apartment near the computers twenty-four hours a day.

Naomi Bartinelli was a very lonely woman.

"Would you like a cigarette?"

"I don't smoke, remember?"

Carter smiled. "Dear me, Naomi, you limit your drinks, you watch your diet, you rarely go out and never entertain, and you don't smoke. Don't you have any vices?"

"I guess not," she said demurely. She then leaned toward him confidentially, her giant breasts threatening to escape their confinement. "I am in a strange business. Let's just say that if I were a gadfly around town, my clients would frown on it."

I'll bet they would, Carter thought, but he managed to keep a straight face.

"I do hope, Naomi, that you have at least one vice. A man can only wait so long, you know."

He could see a slight blush come into her face and then grow. He watched as the rosy hue of embarrassment crept down her neck and infused the wealth of flesh above the bodice of her dress.

Carter fought hard to keep from staring at the hypnotizing phenomenon. He had never seen a woman's breasts blush before.

He decided to push it. "Well?"

"I think," she said haltingly, "that the wait is over."

"Wonderful."

Thankfully the waiter made another appearance, making further comment unnecessary.

The food came, and along with it the wine steward. Carter kept up the act by discusssing a choice of wine at great length with the sommelier. He finally decided on a relatively modest Pommard '67.

Both of them ate heartily, Naomi because of her size, Carter because he needed the food to offset the effect the drinks were beginning to have on him. He had a lot to do this particular evening, and he didn't want to handicap himself.

He checked his watch as they finished dessert and coffee. It was just past ten, time to get down to business.

The restaurant had served its purpose. He had charmed her and wined her and dined her like the cosmopolitan businessman he appeared to be.

"Naomi, will you excuse me for a moment? I must make a call . . . business."

"Of course."

He found a pay phone near the lounges and dialed the number from memory.

Al Garrett picked up on the first ring.

"It's me. Tonight's the night."

"Christ, it's about time!"

"All good things come to those who wait, Al."

"You can say that. At least you're gonna get laid."

"God, you're vulgar. Have you got your gear ready?"

"Hell, yes. When?"

"We're leaving here in about ten minutes. Wait at your hotel until about midnight, then come over."

"Same signal?"

"Right . . . lights on and off twice."

"You're sure about the dog?" Garrett asked, a tremor in his voice.

Carter chuckled. "Let's hope I am."

"Damn you, Carter."

" 'Bye, Al."

They cabbed it uptown to 85th Street and her apartment. It was a twenty story highrise, with a doorman and television security in the hallways and elevators.

That was nothing compared to the three locks on her door and the alarm system she shut off just inside the little entryway. But Carter knew there was still another piece of security Naomi used to guard the secrets of her little business.

He stood, all one hundred and fifty pounds of him, about five feet from Carter, his lips curled back over shiny teeth.

"My," Carter said and swallowed, "what a beautiful Doberman."

"His name is Gordo. Don't worry, he wouldn't touch anybody while I'm in the apartment."

"And when you're not?"

"He's trained to kill." She said it almost as an afterthought.

Gordo was the big reason that Carter had been forced to play Casanova to obtain the information they needed. The AXE break-in boys had figured out how to breach nearly all the security without Naomi Bartinelli knowing they had been there.

Gordo the Doberman had been the stumbling block.

"Go on in, Nick, it's all right."

"You're sure?"

"Of course," she giggled. "Give me your coat."

He did, and approached Gordo. "Would you mind telling him to cover up his teeth?"

"Gordo."

Amazing. The stump of a tail started to wag, and the tongue lolled out to do a number on Carter's hand. His fingers were dripping by the time Naomi moved in behind him and molded her big body against his back.

Carter turned around, and she shifted a little on her toes to bring her lips to his.

She didn't have to lift far.

Her tongue forced its way between his lips, and the wealth of her breasts pressed hotly against his chest.

The fire started building within his body immediately, but it was matched by the sudden knowledge that all her caution and shyness had been thrown to the winds.

"You don't fool around once you make up your mind, do you, Naomi."

"No. I've been waiting too long."

"Where's the bedroom?"

"There."

"And the bar?"

"There."

"Why don't you just slip off your . . . shoes, prop a pillow against the headboard, and get comfortable?" he suggested casually. "I'll fix the drinks. What would you like?"

"Just a Perrier and lime for me," she said, then pecked him again on the lips. "I don't want to dull my senses."

With a little laugh she was gone, and Carter headed for the bar. Gordo trailed along with him, watchful, but he was rubbing Carter's leg, and the tail was now going like crazy.

"Nice Gordo, nice doggie."

The tongue soaked his hand again.

Carter checked out the apartment while he poured and mixed. He had got a glance into the bedroom where Naomi had gone. It wasn't tiny, but it wasn't large enough to be the master suite either.

The small bar served as a room divider between a dining alcove and a large sunken living room. There were two exits on the opposite side of the living room, one with louvered doors and one at the end of a short hall.

Carter guessed kitchen and master bedroom suite.

Behind that second door would be Naomi Bartinelli's office, and the computers.

The dog padded at his heels as he walked down the hall and into the first bedroom.

She was exactly as Carter had suggested, propped against the headboard with her head on a pillow and her shoes off. He had thought that maybe, just maybe, she would have overcome all her shyness and stripped.

But she hadn't. Instead, she lay there looking more like an overgrown, frightened teenager than a widowed woman of around thirty.

Thankfully, Gordo flopped at the foot of the bed, and Carter handed Naomi the Perrier.

"To tonight," he toasted.

"Yes."

Carter watched her drink over the rim of his own glass. Fully a third of the sparkling liquid went down her throat.

That was good.

The depressant he had put in the drink would take almost an hour to work slowly through her system. Her drowsiness would feel natural, and most of it she would attribute to the sex.

"I guess you can see that I'm a little nervous. I can't hide my feelings very well."

Carter stared down at her upturned face, the full lips parted invitingly. The dim light of a single lamp had softened the coarseness of her full face and made it almost pretty. He could see the flush in her cheeks, and her eyes had a look of innocence and vulnerability.

"There's no rush," he said, setting his glass on the night table and sliding onto the bed beside her.

She drank again, gulping another third of the laced Perrier in her nervousness.

Then, breathing a bit rapidly, she put aside the glass and turned to him in open anticipation.

"I've got so damn little to offer a man, really . . . just my body."

Carter experienced a sudden rush of compassion for this buxom woman.

But then he remembered that she was the daughter of one hood and the widow of another. She ran an international information business that dealt in death and terrorism as if they were commodities like toothpaste or breakfast cereal.

And she knew damned well what she was doing.

"There are a lot of women, Naomi, who would give anything to have a body like yours," Carter murmured softly.

"Yeah, I know," she sighed. "They should have the trouble this body has gotten me into."

He reached out to her, and she came quickly into his arms. Her body felt massive, both solid and soft, both firm and pliable. The lips were warm and full as well as moist and easily parted.

He could not help but contrast this quivering, yielding woman in his arms with the hellcat she would become if she knew the real reason he was in her bed and she was in his arms.

He let his lips linger at length and then, when he lifted them from hers, a low, mewling sound came from her throat.

"Nice, so nice."

"It'll get better," he growled, her body starting to do things to his.

He slid his head down, resting it on the soft exposure of her breasts, cupping them to pillow his face. He felt the spark of desire being kindled in him as she reached behind herself and unzipped her dress to the waist.

She shrugged out of her shoulder straps to reveal the overflowing creaminess of her breasts. Carter's thirst for them increased as she reached behind to unfasten her bra.

"Wonderful," he muttered, fondling them, testing their snowy softness, lowering his head to gently kiss their pristine whiteness.

She shivered pleasurably under his touch, her eyes half closed, her pink-ringed nipples beginning to rise. "Oh, Nick, squeeze me. Squeeze me as hard as you can."

He complied, squeezing the massive breasts until he was certain he would hurt her, certain that she would cry out in pain at any second.

But her only response was a series of deep moans and little cries of pleasure. "Oh, yes, Nick. More!"

Carter gave way to the growing hunger inside his belly and fastened his mouth to her swollen nipples.

"Yes, yes, bite me. Bite me hard!" she rasped hoarsely, her hands guiding his lips from nipple to nipple, her breathing ragged.

He fed his hunger in silence as she wriggled the dress the rest of the way off her body. Then she was attacking his clothes with quick, deft hands.

Soft moans came from deep within her, and she sank further and further into the mattress, mashing his face to her breasts. After what seemed an interminable time, she emitted a long moan and shuddered, gently pushing him from her.

"Wait, honey."

Carter caught his breath and steadied his senses as she slid from the bed. He watched the pantyhose slide down her long legs. His blood quickened at the sight of her in the filmy panties that only made a gesture toward covering the wide expanse of her flaring hips.

Then, with her breasts swaying pendulously and a quick smile playing across her lips, she stripped the final garment from her sumptuous body.

The legs were heavy and powerful, the hips ample and polished with a film of perspiration. Her belly was rounded provocatively and still showed the imprint of the elastic in the panties.

"Okay?" she asked timorously.

"C'mere."

She slithered to him, and Carter rolled between her thighs.

A strangled cry erupted from her lips at the moment of possession. Almost immediately, her mouth opened and her breathing became ragged as her face flushed.

He paused for a moment, and she shuddered at the delay. When he moved again, she met him with a great surge of her massive body. Her hips moved against him hungrily and expertly. Her arms tugged him deep into the circle of her warm flesh.

It was a fiercely contested coupling. Carter knew that she was trying to prove something to him, but at that point he cared little. She had goaded him with her body to match her sensual frenzy, and he responded, finding her sudden pagan abandon contagious.

With a growl from deep within his chest, he drove her ahead of him toward the end. Her passion was reaching the stage of delirium as she redoubled her efforts, jerking and bucking, trying to consume him completely.

At last, in one monumental convulsion, her lusty body collapsed in a quaking mass of satiated flesh. Carter held to her, not stopping until, seconds later, the end came for him as well.

He waited several moments, then rolled to her side.

"Naomi . . . ?"

Silence.

He moved back to her. The pulse was even, the breathing normal and steady.

She was out cold.

He pulled on his trousers and padded into the living room. He flipped the main lights on and off once, waited a few seconds, repeated the action, and then noticed that Gordo's big body was rubbing against his legs.

The third cabinet he opened in the kitchen gave him a handful of dog biscuits. He dropped one into the Doberman's gaping maw and returned to the living room and front door.

Al Garrett was waiting with a frown on his round face. He wore the uniform of one of New York's finest.

"Any trouble?"

"Naw, told the doorman I had to check the roof. Peeping Tom complaints from some residents of other buildings. Jesus."

"He's like a big baby," Carter said, sticking another biscuit between Gordo's gleaming teeth. "He wouldn't hurt a fly."

"Oh, yeah? Let's hope he won't hurt little fat men dressed up like cops."

"C'mon, this way!"

The master bedroom suite-cum-office was locked. It took Carter fifteen seconds flat to pick the two locks on the door, and they were inside.

"Wow," Garrett exclaimed when Carter flipped on the lights, "this ain't no home computer center."

"The lady's no hobbyist," Carter said. "Let's get to it."

A moment later, Garrett had the room humming. "Kill that telex. We don't need it, and it might wake her up."

Carter knew that nothing was going to stir Naomi Bartinelli, but he killed the clacking machine anyway.

Al Garrett went to work with a couple of screwdrivers and some black boxes on the back of the machines.

He pulled off a plate, behind which was a plastic-enclosed scrambler. "This is her security system," he explained as he worked. "I'll rig it so we can bypass it right at the source—here—and then with the additional modem I'm going to install, we can intercept as well as decode everything she sends or receives."

"What do you have to do?"

"Cut and resolder these wires, and then put in the alternate modem. Shouldn't take more than a half hour."

Carter lit a custom-blended cigarette and paced.

Twenty-five minutes later, Garrett was finished in the back of the machines and was sitting at the console, his fingers flying and his eyes darting from one screen to the other.

"I think I've got it."

"How long till you can break her system?" Carter asked.

"Three days, maybe less if she runs a lot of traffic."

"Good. Anything else?"

"That's it."

They shut the system down, resecured the room, and moved back to the front door.

"You'll call the man?"

Garrett nodded and moved away down the hall.

The man was David Hawk, head of AXE, whom Carter knew would be waiting in the Dupont Circle offices of AXE's front, Amalgamated Press and Wire Services.

Carter closed and relocked the door, then headed back to the bedroom.

In his mind he was already composing the sad story he would tell Naomi Bartinelli in the morning over breakfast.

"I shouldn't be gone more than three weeks, maybe four. I'll call you the moment I get back to New York. Perhaps we can take a little time off together somewhere.''

But as he rolled wearily into bed beside her, Carter knew that the only time off Naomi Bartinelli would be taking would be spent in a federal prison for women, courtesy of the FBI.

That is, after Carter's mission was completed and AXE turned her file over to them.

TWO

Ali Maumed Kashmir lived in a twenty-five-room mansion in the Great Bay area of the Jersey shore. The house was an uneasy melding of Mediterranean and Colonial American elements, and rested on thirty-two wooded acres with approximately five hundred feet of private beach fronting the property.

On that night, the small marina, the pool area, the mansion, and the long, winding gravel drive leading up to it were festooned with dozens of sparkling chandeliers, muted lanterns, and blazing torches.

A limousine announced itself at the tall wrought-iron gates. They swung open, and the big car glided noiselessly through.

In the cavernous rear seat sat a statuesque woman with dark brown eyes and raven black hair, a brown cigarette held in one black-gloved hand.

She was tall, with a proud figure. A black and yellow print dress lovingly covered her tapering curves.

Her name was Carlotta Polti. She had been born in Florence, Italy, and was now employed in Rome as a feature writer for one of the country's more leftist-leaning magazines. For the last two years, Carlotta Polti had also been a member in good standing of La Amicizia di Libertà Italiana, one of the more militant guerrilla/terrorist groups in her native country.

She had worked hard in those two years to ingratiate herself and rise through the ranks in the Friendship for Italian Liberty group. But being a magazine writer and a guerrilla were not her true occupations.

Her true employment was as a top undercover agent for the antiterrorist arm of Italy's internal security organization, the SID.

The car came to a halt in front of the mansion's deep veranda, and the chauffeur was immediately at the door.

Outside the car, the woman seemed even taller, with small, taut breasts, womanly hips, and miles of tapering, perfectly proportioned legs. Though she was only twenty-seven, her face had a hardness far beyond her years, and her smoldering dark eyes were as sullen as they were erotic.

"I will have your bags taken care of, *signorina*."

"*Grazie.*"

Carlotta ascended the stairs, and halfway across the veranda a servant in a tuxedo opened the door and bowed her through. Inside, she announced herself to a butler, also immaculately dressed. Only a trained eye such as hers could have spotted the telltale bulges under the jackets of the doorman and the butler.

Both men were armed, as had been the chauffeur and the guard tending the gate.

She had just passed through the tall archway into a large, high-ceilinged room, when Ali Maumed Kashmir appeared before her.

Carlotta took in his lean, powerful frame in one glance. In the year since they had last met face to face, she detected few changes other than more gray in the hair and an added inch or so in the belly.

"Ah, Carlotta, has it been a year? You are more beautiful than ever!"

Her smile, as he kissed her hand, was genuinely warm. She had been practicing it for years.

"I hope the drive down from Manhattan was pleasant?"

"Of course. It is a very comfortable car."

Kashmir shrugged, the smile on his face almost a leer. "Capitalism does have its rewards. Come, I will introduce you to the other guests."

They moved across the large room toward the bar, with Kashmir introducing Carlotta as an Italian journalist and an old friend from Rome.

Both were only half truths.

Her only prior meeting with Kashmir had been to conclude a purchase of small arms for the Libertà. Eventually, those arms—through an anonymous tip—found their way into SID hands instead of terrorist guerrilla apartments. But the contact had been made, and that had been Carlotta's real reason more than the actual arms.

The guests were an assortment of nearby neighbors, show people from New York, and business acquaintances of Kashmir. The business acquaintances were most likely legitimate. Some of the man's businesses were legitimate, such as the import and distribution of carpets and trinkets from Morocco, gems from Thailand, and fine china and glassware from Europe.

Neither these endeavors nor his inheritance, however, could account for the style of life he enjoyed, or the vast sums held for him in banks in Switzerland and Liechtenstein.

It was the brokering of vast quantities of illegal arms that made Ali Maumed Kashmir a very wealthy man.

At last they reached the bar.

"What would you like?"

"Campari."

A glass was instantly thrust into her hand. Ali stood smiling at her, adopting the mannered, hipshot pose that seemed to be his trademark as a playboy.

Her eyes made a lazy arc around the room as she sipped her drink. "You live well, Ali."

"The fruits of my hard labor."

"And your friends seem rather . . . passé."

He shrugged and spoke in a lowered voice. "They are part of this aspect of my life . . . a very necessary part."

"They look like St. Moritz in the winter, Biarritz or the Lido in summer, yachts converted from destroyer escorts, polo—"

"All of that and more," he interrupted, letting a little sneer dance over his thin lips as he, too, surveyed the group. "I was born to it. Sometimes it bores me, sometimes it amuses me. But an outsider, like yourself, is a welcome change . . . particularly when so beautiful."

"I didn't come here to be an adornment to your party, Ali."

"Of course not," he sighed. "But you must admit it is an ideal environment in which to discuss our business. These idiots would never see anything beyond their own noses."

"When?"

"Soon, when everyone is fully enjoying themselves. I'll let you know. For now, excuse me. Relax and enjoy yourself, my dear. They can be quite amusing."

Carlotta watched him move through the crowd, and felt fingers of warning slither up and down her spine. Kashmir was a master at survival. If he had any idea of the real reason she was here, or the fact that, at that very moment, an American agent, Nick Carter, and several of his cohorts were lying offshore ready to storm the house on her signal, Carlotta knew her life would be worth nothing.

While she waited for some sign from Kashmir, she moved

casually through the group of laughing and chattering people, carefully watching her host from the corner of her eye. He was now in a small group by the fireplace, talking to an American screen star. She, in turn, was holding court for five other men who hung on her every word.

Carlotta recognized several other faces in the room from magazines and newspapers around the world, and she let a smile curl her lip.

Most of the people were highly visible. Many of them were written about almost weekly, somewhere, and often the story was accompanied by a photograph.

Not so Kashmir. To her knowledge, he had never been photographed, and very few people he dealt with had ever met him face to face.

Carlotta knew that one of the reasons she had been so honored was the fact of Kashmir's lechery. He had tried several times during their previous meeting to lure her into his bed, without success. This time, when she had contacted him, he had been only too happy to accede to her suggestion that she come to him in the U.S.

Carlotta found herself talking to an aging Wall Street broker, while constantly shifting her eyes toward Kashmir. The man beamed at her, giving vent to his profoundest thoughts on humanity, on the direction the world was headed, and the deplorable sexual freedom among the young.

At the end of his diatribe, he gently pinched her bottom and strolled away.

"Signorina?"

It was the bull-like butler with the bulge under his left armpit.

"Yes?"

"He would like to see you in his office. It is the first door to the right at the top of the stairway."

Carlotta nodded, handed him her glass, and moved across

the room. In her mind she went over the shopping list of arms she had prepared for Ali Maumed Kashmir, the merchant of death.

"Hadley, are you in place?"

"Right. I'm with Chris, about a mile out from the gate."

"Good. Barzoni? . . . Hal?"

"Barzoni here. I'm on the left perimeter. I can see right down into the compound."

"This is Hal. I'm in place on the right and on the hill."

"Check," Carter replied. "She's inside. Step down and rest easy. It's probably going to be a long night."

The replies squawked back at him through the small hand-held radio. Carter snapped it to "receive," belted it, and turned to the other three men in the launch.

Two of them were in black rubber wet suits like himself. The third man was dressed in dungarees, a black shirt, and a dark jacket. He was the pilot of the launch that now bobbed in the middle of Great Bay. His name was Harris, and like the launch, he had been borrowed from the Coast Guard for the operation.

"Ted, Marko . . . have you both got it, or do you want to go over it again?"

"Not much to it, really," replied the taller of the two men. "Marko and I take the marina and perimeter guards, while you go for the power source to shut off the fence."

Carter nodded. "Don't waste anybody unless it's an absolute necessity. We don't want a bloodbath if we can help it."

"What makes a necessity?"

"Anybody who tries to give an alarm," Carter replied, then stepped through the launch's hatch into the small cabin.

It had originally contained a galley, a table, and a couple of bunks. The galley remained, but the bunks and the table had been removed and replaced with communications equipment.

One small receiver between two larger ones glowed with a pulsing green light. When Carlotta Polti had word from Kashmir that the order could be filled, and the pickup and payment was cleared, that light would shift to red.

It was their signal to go.

Carter lit a cigarette and sat down to watch and wait.

"This is a very long and involved list," Kashmir said, looking over the notes he had made in an undecipherable scrawl. "Are you planning on overthrowing the entire government this time?"

"You merely broker the arms, Ali. You and I know that you don't give a damn what we do with them once they are paid for."

"*Touché.*"

"Can you supply?"

His attention returned to the notes. The eyes were cold now, calculating profit. Gone was the sneering, practiced smile of the playboy jet-setter.

"The sniper rifles, the L39AIs . . ."

"Yes?"

"They are extremely difficult to come by, especially in these quantities."

Carlotta inhaled deeply on a cigarette and let the twin spumes of smoke shoot from her nostrils before replying. "Then I suppose they will be more expensive."

"Quite," he replied with a thin-lipped smile. "Would the new British Parker-Hale .222 do, if they are available? It has the same velocity but without the overpenetration."

She seemed to think a great deal on this. Actually, the quantity and the nature of the arms made very little difference. They would only be used as bait and pawns anyway, and, like the earlier shipment from Kashmir, they would never make their way into the hands of La Amicizia di Libertà Italiana.

Of course, she did not want Kashmir to know that.

"Yes, we would prefer the AIs, but we would accept the Parker-Hales as substitutes."

"The plastique, the submachine guns, and the fitted laser sights will be no problem." Kashmir looked up, his eyes boring into hers. "Do you have your own end-use certificate, or do I supply one?"

"That would depend on the place of delivery."

"I would prefer Amsterdam. Brussels is very dangerous right now."

"Then we will need a certificate."

He nodded. "You will take delivery personally?"

"Yes."

"Very well. Now . . . payment."

"Half on contract, half on delivery. The first half through Swiss accounts, the second half in cash."

"Swiss francs?"

"If you so desire."

"I do," Kashmir said, uncoiling from his chair and coming around the desk. "It will take about an hour to get a reply. In the meantime, why don't you rejoin the party?"

Carlotta stood and walked with him to the door.

"My chauffeur tells me that you brought down your bags with you."

"Wasn't that your suggestion? . . . That I stay the night?"

"Of course. I'm just rather surprised that you have decided to do so. The last time we met, I must say you were rather cold toward my . . . suggestions."

He had stopped, turning her body to his. Now he was

slowly running his hands up and down her back and gently moving his lower body against hers.

Carlotta felt a shudder of revulsion begin its surge through her from his touch, and suppressed it.

"That was last time, Ali. This is *this* time."

His dark eyes flashed. "I am elated. With a client so beautiful, it will be a joy to mix a bit of pleasure with business."

She met his gaze evenly. "Just don't forget that the primary purpose of this visit is business."

"Of course. Perhaps later, once our little transaction is concluded, we could indulge in a little moonlight swim? . . . Nude, of course."

"Hardly," she said with a chuckle. "I don't make a spectacle of myself, and I'm not interested in orgies."

"You mean the other guests?"

"Yes."

Kashmir laughed. "There is a simple solution to that. My little party will break up early, and they will all be sent home."

Carlotta forced herself not to let the relief register on her face. If everything went according to plan in the wee hours of the morning, it was imperative that there be no innocent, legitimate people around to muddy up the waters.

"Well?"

"I think a midnight swim—nude, of course—would be exciting."

"Excellent!"

He let her out the door and quickly walked back to the wall behind his desk. A deft twist of a small piece of molding, and a panel in the wall slid open just wide enough to let him pass through.

The room was small, just large enough for a computer, a

desk, and a telephone setup.

Kashmir activated the machine, and when it was warmed up sufficiently, dialed the special Manhattan number. When the modem clicked in, he began to send.

Naomi Bartinelli rarely drank. By the light from the lamp on her night table, she saw that she had already consumed half of the bottle of sherry next to it.

It had been four nights since she had wantonly given herself to the tall, handsome man she had met in the Oak Room of the Plaza Hotel. He had departed the next morning, saying that he wouldn't be able to see her for at least a few weeks, some flimsy excuse of a business trip.

She knew it was a lie. She would never see him again. It was the story of her life.

Oddly, she wondered if the almost two million dollars in her accounts would have impressed him as much as her body had obviously impressed him. Bodies were transitory; money was solid.

No, she would never see him again, and it was a shame. He had been a wonderful lover. But perhaps it was just as well. How would she ever explain to him the source of her wealth?

That was why Naomi had dipped so deeply into the bottle of sherry. Once again she was envisioning herself as a lonely, rich old lady one day.

She clicked the tiny, concealed switch on the light that would trip the breaker so the bulb would stay lit and moved through the living room to her office.

It took her a couple of minutes longer than usual to work the locks. Her eyes didn't seem to want to focus.

At last she was in the room and the equipment was humming. Seated, she typed in a ''GO AHEAD,'' and the word ''JASMINE'' appeared on one of the screens.

All the codes and security passwords of her various clients

had long ago been thoroughly memorized, so even in her slightly befogged state, Naomi was immediately able to reply.

"ALPHA ZONE."

"ACKNOWLEDGE . . . ORDER . . . JASMINE TO OAKHURST."

"PASSWORD?"

"DECIBEL."

"GO AHEAD."

A long series of numbers and more coded words appeared on the screen, ending with the plain language "PLEASE ACKNOWLEDGE ONE HOUR."

"AGREE."

The screen went blank, and Naomi reached for the telephone to gain access to a transatlantic line.

For the second time that evening, Carlotta walked up the stairs. Behind her, the party was already breaking up. With any luck, all the guests would be off the grounds in less than a half hour's time.

"Come in, my dear."

Carlotta eased herself into the same high-backed leather chair and accepted the light he offered.

"The merchandise is available. Half of the L39AIs you requested. I can fill out the order with Parker-Hales."

"Good. And delivery?"

"This is Monday. Shall we say Friday? In Amsterdam?"

"Fine. How will the contact be made?"

"Come, come, my dear. You know I can't give you that information until you are there and the money has been transferred."

"Of course." She smiled, mashing out her cigarette. "And now the price."

"Two hundred and twenty thousand. That includes the

end-use certificate and delivery to your point of departure.''

"Very well," Carlotta replied, standing. "I'll contact our people in Switzerland in the morning."

Kashmir moved in close to her, sliding his arms around her waist and cupping her buttocks in his hands. "I'll send off the verification and meet you by the pool in a half hour. That is, if you haven't changed your mind . . .''

Carlotta allowed her body to melt against his as Carter's words ran through her mind:

Stay with him, Carlotta . . . from the time you send the go, stay with him. He's surely got a way out of there for emergencies. Stay glued to him and make sure he doesn't slip us. The entire operation depends on nailing Kashmir so he can't show up later and ruin everything. If something happens when we go in that warns him, make sure he doesn't get away!

His lips covered hers, and Carlotta didn't jerk away when his tongue began to probe inside her mouth.

"We will be beautiful together, don't you think, my dear?"

"Yes, beautiful."

"The pool? A half hour?"

"A half hour," she said, turning and walking quickly toward the door.

THREE

The pool was octagonal in shape and enclosed in a bubble dome. There were muted lights glowing beneath its surface. Since the patio lights and most of the lights in the rear rooms of the mansion had been extinguished, the only illumination was from the pool itself.

Kashmir was already there, standing on the low board at the far end, his tall, well-muscled body suitless.

Carlotta waved and approached the edge of the pool. Her long, black hair was braided and wrapped around her head. She wore a black silk robe that hugged her body and ended mid-thigh to reveal the astonishing length of her statuesque limbs. A small black clutch bag was in her right hand. Inside the bag was a package of cigarettes and a lighter.

Built into the base of the lighter was a tiny homing device that, when activated, would send a lone signal approximately one mile.

"It's a beautiful evening," Ali called, looking up through the dome at the dark, star-dotted sky.

"Yes, it is. Is everything settled for Friday?"

"Quite. Our business is completed."

He arced from the board and cut the water cleanly. As he swam toward her, Carlotta put a cigarette between her lips and thumbed the lighter. Just before she placed it, and the bag, on a poolside table, she twisted the lighter's base, activating the beeper.

Ali's head surfaced just beneath her. His teeth gleamed in a broad smile, and his eyes searched the robe for a telltale sign that she was wearing a bathing suit beneath it.

"Are you coming in?"

"Of course." Carlotta tugged at the belt. The robe parted, and with a shrug of her shoulders it shimmied downward to puddle at her feet.

"Beautiful," Ali sighed.

The pool lights sifting through the water created dancing shadows on the supple curves and hollows of her nude body. Her buttocks were firm and rounded, her waist slim, and her thighs sleek. She sported an all-over tan, and when she moved to toss the cigarette away, her skin in the light took on a golden glow.

"We will go slowly," Ali said. "I want to enjoy you leisurely."

"Yes, let's take a very long time, Ali."

Carlotta slipped into the water, keeping her face a bland mask as his arms went around her.

Carter bounded back up to the deck. "Ted, Marko . . . it's a go!"

The three men moved aft. Within seconds, they had buckled webbed belts around their middles. Attached to the belts were Fairbairn commando knives and two waterproof bags with silenced pistols and spare clips.

Hopefully, a knife and a handgun would be all they would need. Everything had to happen close and quiet.

Carter lifted the radio from his belt and barked into it. "Hadley?"

"Yo!"

"It's a go. You know the time sequence."

"Right."

"Barzoni? . . . Hal?"

"Here."

"On."

"Come on down to the fence line. You'll know the power's off when the lights go."

"Check."

Carter killed the radio and stored it inside the wet suit jumper before turning to the men beside him. "All right, let's go."

The three of them slipped off the fantail of the launch, one veering right, one left, and Carter heading straight into the dock.

The Ford sedan stopped just outside the gates. The headlights blinked out, leaving only the parking lights as the driver's door opened and a man in a loud sport shirt got out.

The guard slipped his hand inside his jacket and moved to the center of the gates.

"I think my buddy and I are lost. Do you know the right road to Midvail?"

"Never heard of it," the guard replied.

"It's right here on this map, but I can't find the right road running to it."

A hand holding a map was thrust through the grillwork. Instinctively, the guard reached for it. His fingers had barely folded over the paper when the other man's hand was at his throat.

He struggled for a count of three before his body went limp.

The guard had barely crumpled to the drive before the second man was out of the car and on its roof. Like a gymnast, he leaped to the hood and from there to the top of the gates. Effortlessly, he flipped upward. For a split second his body was outlined against the night sky, and then his soft-soled sneakers crunched on the gravel inside the gate.

Seconds later, the guard's body had been dragged to the side and the gates were swinging open.

Without a sound, both men faded into the trees and moved toward the house. By the time they had rejoined in a clump of trees across from the wide front veranda, two roving sentries had met the same fate as the gate guard.

Carter surfaced beneath the pier and made his way along its length to the boathouse. As he came up the ladder, he heard voices. The door was cracked against the night's humid heat, revealing two men inside. They were at a table, pushing checkers back and forth across a board.

As he moved to the door, Carter tugged Wilhelmina, his 9mm Luger, from the waterproof bag on his belt. Deftly, he checked the silencer and levered a shell into the chamber.

Both men got instant owl eyes as he kicked the door the rest of the way open and stepped inside, the Luger up and at arm's length in both hands in front of his face.

"Don't make a sound or a move or it's your last."

There was a two-second stunned pause, and then the one on the right moved. His hand flew to his belt, and then the arm came up in an arc.

He was incredibly fast. The Fairbairn in his hand was just like the one in Carter's belt, and from the way the arm was cocked, Carter knew he was accurate.

The throwing arm was just cocked, a millisecond before release, when the Killmaster pumped two slugs into his chest from the Luger. Crimson spots appeared two inches apart on his T-shirt, and his body flew backward from the impact of the 9mm slugs.

Number two was just as brave and just as quick.

He started coming in on the front side, his hamlike hands curled for a kill, and then sidestepped to Carter's right.

Carter got off one shot that bloodied his ear before impact. He felt one of the big hands chop his wrist, sending the Luger flying from his grasp to land on the floor in the corner.

A chop came up with sledgehammer power toward Carter's head. It glanced off his temple without claiming full force as the Killmaster rolled with the swing to duck away. Carter made a full swinging turn away and then brought the back of his forearm around in a wide arc, completing the circle and connecting with a thudding sound against the man's face and head.

Bone snapped in the man's cheek, and his eyes popped wide in sudden surprise. He fell back, smashing hard against the wall, his splintered jaw moving but no sound coming from his throat.

"Quit now," Carter rasped, "and you'll still be breathing tomorrow."

No way.

He came back like a bull. Carter ducked under the rush and brought a knee hard up into the other's groin. The blow was met with a gagging groan of pain, and the body bent forward to stumble in a tight circle.

Carter stepped away and chopped the side of his hand down across the back of the man's neck.

He went down like wheat under a scythe.

Carter checked the first one. He was dead, and the other one would be out for hours. Even if he did wake up sooner than that, he would have a hard time navigating. And it would be too late anyway.

Outside, Carter dropped from the pier to the beach and moved up to the low stone breaker wall. He vaulted it and, shunning the path, moved up the hill through the formal gardens that vied evenly with lawn from the rear of the house to the water.

Fifty yards up, Marko came in from his right.

"Two in the boathouse," Carter said. "You?"

"I got mine."

"Let's go."

Another twenty-five yards brought them to a small steel shed. The door was unlocked. Carter darted in, the other agent at his heels already fanning a penlight around the interior.

Carter explained in quick, staccato sentences.

"This is the main-line power box. Kill this switch, jam your shorter here, then turn the power back on. After the blackout comes, the emergency generator will kick on in about thirty seconds."

"Got it."

"You kill the emergency here. You'd better jam it, too, just in case someone gets by us."

"Roger."

Carter moved out and started the rest of the way up the hill toward the house.

By now, Hadley and Chris would be through the gate and ready in front. Marko had got the inside perimeter guard on the right and was in the power shed. Ted would hopefully have cleared the inside of the fence on the left and, like Carter, would be moving toward the house.

With any luck, Barzoni and Hal would have dropped the outside sentries, and were already setting up with sniper rifles on the high ground commanding the rear all the way to the water.

Their orders: *If anybody breaks free from the house, drop them.*

Carter skirted the pool with a quick glance. He saw the two dark heads bobbing on the surface near the shallow end and grinned to himself.

Good girl. Carlotta was sticking close to Kashmir.

Idly, he wondered *how* close.

Across from the service entrance, he dropped into a crouch and pulled a pair of night goggles over his eyes.

With any luck, it would all be over in another fifteen minutes.

The back of her neck and shoulders were out of the water. Carlotta could feel perspiration beading that part of her body.

How much longer? she wondered.

She knew she couldn't deny Kashmir's lust much more. She could feel the evidence of it straining on her thigh.

He was like an octopus, all hands and fingers, clutching at her breasts and buttocks, groping between her thighs.

"Do you tease me for pleasure, Carlotta?"

"Of course not," she replied, managing a coy smile. "I do it to heighten the anticipation."

"My anticipation is heightened enough," he hissed, pushing her hard against the edge of the pool.

He used his own knees to pry hers apart. Carlotta found his hips with her hands and managed to tug him toward her yet push him away at the last second.

"You are a bitch."

"Of course I am. It adds to the excitement."

"Damn you," he growled, then lunged forward, breaking her grip.

She tightened her muscles as she felt his attempted entrance, but she knew that it was only a matter of seconds.

And then everything went dark.

Kashmir's body tensed. For a second Carlotta thought he

would leave her and climb from the pool. She curled one hand around his neck and brought the other to the tight coil of her hair, just in case.

"What happened?"

"A power failure," he replied.

Suddenly the lights came back on, but for only a flicker, and again the pool was plunged into darkness.

Above her, Carlotta could see Kashmir's eyes narrow in the moonlight and a tense expectation enter his features.

For the moment, he had forgotten his lust.

"The emergency generator should come on soon."

The words had barely left his lips when once again illumination filtered up through the water.

His lips curved in a leering smile. "Now, you beautiful bitch, I'll have you."

Carter watched the sweep-second hand of his watch. When fifty seconds had elapsed since the emergency generator's kick-in, he started toward the house in a crouching sprint.

Halfway there, the lights went off again for the last time.

Carter hit the door at a dead run. Just beyond it was a small alcove, and then the kitchen. A big, broad-shouldered ape in a tuxedo was standing in the middle of the room by a butcher block. He had managed to get one camp lantern lit and was working on a second one.

Carter's knee scraped a chair, and the ape whirled at the sound.

The Killmaster didn't pause a step in his run. He lowered a shoulder into the tuxedoed gut and jammed the man up against a big double-door refrigerator.

Foul breath wheezed by Carter's ear as the other man fell back toward him, his hands instinctively groping beneath his dark jacket.

Carter sliced him once across the neck with the barrel and

silencer of the Luger, and then gave him another chop on the way down.

Off the kitchen was a small dining room, and off that the great room. Carter hit that door just as Hadley and Chris came through the front door, dragging the unconscious body of the chauffeur between them.

"I got one in the kitchen," Carter rasped.

"And this is two. Two to go."

Hadley and his partner dropped the man between them and moved on into the pitch-black room. Just as they passed into a stream of moonlight coming through one of the room's tall, cathedral-type windows, Carter spotted movement to his left at the top of the stairs.

He dropped to one knee and rolled his gaze up. Through the night goggles, he saw a machine pistol come up from one man's side as a second bolted down the stairs.

"Roll!" Carter barked.

Hadley and Chris dived. Carter got off two quick shots. Both were hits, but not quick enough.

The machine pistol in the man's hands began chattering, sending a spray of slugs across the floor and up the wall to shatter the huge window.

"Shit," Carter hissed. "You guys okay?"

"Chris caught one in the thigh."

"Take care of him. I'll go after the other one!"

Carter raced toward the rear of the house, hoping Carlotta was as good as he thought she was.

When the emergency generator went out, Ali Kashmir's ardor cooled with it.

"Something is wrong."

"Forget it," Carlotta said, tugging him back to her with her left hand on his neck. "You said it is only a power failure."

"No, the emergency—"

"Come to me, Ali," she cooed. "I am ready."

He started to settle back between her thighs, but she could tell from the tenseness in his body and the wariness in his eyes that any sound or movement around him would send him into flight.

He opened his lips to speak, but Carlotta silenced him by crushing her lips over his mouth. At the same time, she arched her hips, rubbing herself against him.

By the time he had pulled his lips from hers and lifted his head, the stiletto was out of sight behind his shoulder.

"I'd better go check. Someone should be—"

The night erupted. There was a loud stutter of gunfire, and suddenly one of the huge cathedral windows shattered outward, sending fragments of glass over the stone patio.

"Ali . . . Ali, we are overcome!"

Above her head, Carlotta saw a figure dash from the house. There was a spurt of flame from the hill to her right, and the man staggered.

"Damn!" Kashmir cried as the man pitched forward and slid nearly to the pool's edge.

Ali's eyes rolled down to meet Carlotta's, and in that instant he knew.

He was reaching for her throat when Carlotta wound her legs tightly around his back and snapped her feet together. She still clutched his neck and her left hand and, with her finger, counted the bumps of his upper vertabrae.

He managed to curl his fingers up from the back of her neck and close them over her throat.

"Bitch!" he gasped as their struggles rolled them underwater.

Carlotta could feel his fingers tightening. She found the part of his spine she wanted and placed the needlelike point of the stiletto an eighth of an inch into the flesh.

At the sharp prick of pain, his fingers instantly left her throat and reached to stop the thrust.

He was too late.

She placed both hands on the hilt of the stiletto and, with all the power in her arms, pushed the blade down, toward her own breast sliding beneath him.

It was a sure hit. The spine severed neatly, and his body went limp against her.

By the time Carter reached the edge of the pool, she was standing waist-deep in the water, her small breasts heaving.

Beside her, Ali Kashmir floated facedown, a trickle of blood seeping from around the hilt of the stiletto protruding from his neck.

"You all right?"

She rolled her head up to face him. Her eyes were clear and her lower lip quivered only slightly.

"Yes. It couldn't be helped."

Carter grasped Kashmir's body by the hair and pulled it toward the side. The stiletto was his own, the second of Nick Carter's deadly friends, nicknamed Hugo.

He pulled the blade out, swished it in the water to remove the red residue, and slipped it into his belt.

Then he picked up Carlotta's black silk wrap from the cement with his right hand and held out his left to the woman.

"He's no great loss. C'mon."

"Al?"

"Yeah," Garrett answered from a motel room approximately five miles from where Carter stood in Ali Kashmir's upstairs office.

"We're secure. Bring it on in!"

"Twenty minutes."

The phone went dead. Carter looked up as Marko entered the room.

"All secure. We'll have the garbage boys take away the stiffs. The others are padded down in the wine cellar."

"How's Chris?"

"He'll be all right. A lot of blood, but nothing severely severed."

"Good."

Marko moved around the desk. "A couple of them were only too happy to talk." He twisted the wall molding, and the panel in the wall slid open.

Carter glanced in quickly and smiled. "Al Garrett will have a ball."

"I'll set up the perimeter guards."

Carter nodded and exited the room with him. Marko went down the stairs, Carter down the hall. He stopped at the second door he came to and knocked.

"Come in."

She was seated at a vanity, a large, European-style bath towel wound around her body. Her eyes caught his in the mirror, but the hand wielding a brush through her long, glossy black tresses didn't stop.

"You still okay?"

"Of course. It's not the first time."

"I didn't think it was."

He stopped the hand and brought it to his lips. Gently, he kissed it.

"You're good."

"Thank you."

"But this is only the beginning."

"I know. Don't worry about me."

"Did you make the call to Rome?"

Carlotta nodded. "I informed Palmori that Kashmir himself would be accompanying me to Amsterdam and would help in the final delivery of the goods in Italy."

"Any static?"

"None. Palmori considers Kashmir a friend of our cause."

"And you're sure none of them will recognize me when the time comes?"

"No one. I am the only one in the Libertà who has had personal contact with Kashmir."

"Good." He checked his watch. It would be dawn in less than an hour. "You'd better get some sleep. We'll drive to Manhattan at around five in the limo. Our plane leaves Kennedy tonight at ten-fifteen."

She nodded and went back to brushing her hair. Her voice stopped Carter just as he reached the door.

"Are you sure your people can keep this place secure for as long as the operation will take?"

"I'm sure," Carter replied. "And Al Garrett will know enough about Ali Kashmir's business within a week to run the whole thing right from that computer in the office."

"What about friends . . . business or personal?"

"Kashmir is on a long business trip. . ." Carter paused, smiling. "Which is partially true."

"And when it breaks in the papers that Ali Kashmir has been imprisoned in Italy for gunrunning and terrorist activities . . .?"

Again Carter smiled. "We have people specially trained to mount and maintain a cover, no matter what may occur. Satisfied?"

"Satisfied, Nick . . ."

"Yes?"

"For what it's worth, I think I'm going to enjoy the rest of the time with you."

"That goes both ways."

He closed the door gently behind him, but not before he got a quick glimpse of Carlotta Polti standing, dropping the towel, and moving toward the bed.

She looked a lot more beautiful in the bedroom than she had in the pool with a dead body floating beside her.

Downstairs, he eyeballed the bottles behind the bar and found the most expensive scotch there. He poured three fingers into a glass and downed it. He doctored four fingers of a second one with ice and was just starting on it when Al Garrett and his entourage of technicians walked through the front door.

"Anybody left alive?"

"A few," Carter replied. "They're in the wine cellar. Marko says a couple of them are very talkative, should you need to know something."

Garrett nodded and turned to the waiting men behind him. "Okay, you guys, spread out and find rooms. As soon as you stow your gear, come on back down here. We'll get started right away. We've got a big company to run."

"How long do you guess this one will take?"

"Only Carter knows that," he said, turning back to Carter.

Carter shrugged. "A month, not more than five weeks. We think the date for the big summit between the KGB and the terrorist groups will be about then. By the way, hands off on the first two bedrooms on the left at the top of the stairs. The lady and I will need those for today."

There were several nods, and the men dispersed. Garrett moved behind the bar and took a healthy slug of sour mash.

"That stuff will kill you," Carter said.

"So will old age and not using seat belts," Garrett replied. "Where is it?"

"Upstairs."

"Let's go."

Garrett dived into the computer and the books of records alongside it as Carter eased in behind the desk. Carter lit a cigarette, took a slug from his drink, and dialed David

Hawk's private Washington number.

"It's me, sir."

"How did it go?"

"Five bad guys wasted along with Kashmir himself. Three stretcher cases with sore heads. They're in the wine cellar. The cleanup boys are on their way to dispose of the deceased."

"And ours?"

"One winged, Chris. It's not serious. He's already on his way to Bethesda."

"How did the Italian lady fare?"

"Like a champ. She killed Kashmir herself."

"Excellent. Then you have no doubts she can carry the rest of it off?"

"None. What do we hear from Rome?"

"Pietro Amani's parole has been denied. We had a little bit to do with that, of course, but it's a known fact that Nicolo Palmori would try to kill him if he were released, so the parole denial is pretty plausible."

"Anything further on the meet? . . . time? . . . place?"

"Nothing. There are rumblings all over the world, so we know it's going to happen. But this operation is still the only real chance we have to find out when and where."

"Good enough," Carter said, downing the last of the scotch in the glass. "Delivery is for Amsterdam, Friday."

"I'll set up means of transportation. Anything else right now?"

"Nothing that I can think of. I'll contact you just before we hit Italy."

"Fine."

No good-byes were said. Sign-off between the head of AXE and his top agent was easily done with a tonal inflection.

Carter moved to the wall panel. Garrett was humming as

his fingers flew over the keys.

"What do you think?"

"Piece of cake. Man, this guy is into everything."

"You're sure you can shoot through Bartinelli to Amsterdam without tipping us?"

"Positive. She must have been off her feed earlier tonight. She transmitted some plain-language stuff, then turned around and sent the same things in code. Helped crack it in minutes."

"I'm going to get some sleep. Roust me about two."

"You got it."

Carter moved into the hall. He paused at Carlotta Polti's door, remembering how she looked when she had dropped that towel.

His knuckles were halfway up to the door panel, when he changed his mind and moved on down the hall to the other bedroom.

Time enough for that later, he thought.

FOUR

Passports at Kennedy were no problem. Carlotta used her own. Carter used Ali Maumed Kashmir's. It was Lebanese, and one of Al Garrett's team had doctored it perfectly with Carter's picture and a stamp that defied proof of falsification.

The KLM 747 lifted off at exactly ten-fifteen, and drinks were placed in front of them the moment they hit cruising altitude.

"Where will we stay in Amsterdam?" Her eyes were clear and bright. The day's uninterrupted rest had done her a world of good.

"The Amstel," Carter replied, "until after the contact is made and everything is set. We'll play it by ear from there."

She sipped her drink thoughtfully. "It will be a long way from Amsterdam to Italy."

Carter nodded. "And even longer from there to . . . God knows where."

"I know." She eased her head back onto the seat, slipped the small plastic earphones of the in-flight entertainment recording to her ears, and closed her eyes as soothing music infused the tiny headset.

Carter retreated into his own thoughts.

His mind ticked off what had already been accomplished and what they hoped to accomplish in the next few weeks.

For the past several months, intelligence services throughout the free world had gotten rumblings that terrorist activities were about to be stepped up. After weeks of piecing together odds and ends of information, rumors, and a few solid facts, it was theorized that the KGB was preparing to jump back into worldwide terrorism with both feet.

Quietly, word had gone out from Number 2 Dzerzhinsky Square—KGB headquarters in Moscow—that Big Daddy himself would like a meeting with terrorist leaders.

Ostensibly, the meeting would be to plot future terrorist thrusts in their respective countries under the guidance of the KGB. It also came to light that an agreement would probably be reached as to the money and arms that Mother Russia would pour into the programs to step up terrorist activities in the West.

When enough facts and figures had been assembled, a team had been put together and a plan formulated. Eventually, the key twist in the plan had been handed over to David Hawk and AXE.

"The end result is fairly simple, N3," Hawk had said, chewing on his cigar and frowning at his top agent across the expanse of his cluttered desk. "We would like to know where and when this meeting will take place."

"And from there?"

"Disrupt it, of course. But more importantly, we'd like to get some concrete proof to hold over the KGB's head that they are indeed sponsoring worldwide terrorism."

"It would be a coup."

"One of the biggest," Hawk growled, flashing a rare, malevolent smile. "We've got a plan that may get you to that meeting."

Pietro Amani was the founder of a once-powerful Italian

guerrilla group called La Amicizia di Libertà Italiana. His life—and his case—was an odd one. As the scion of a wealthy Italian publishing family, it seemed impossible that Amani would become the leader of a group whose sole purpose for being was the overthrow of the very class of which he was an intrinsic member.

But that was indeed the case.

However, Amani was more than a left-wing millionaire. He wanted to go down in history as Italy's Fidel Castro, the so-called liberator of his people. In so doing, Amani had spent nearly all his fortune trying to buy the place in history he coveted so much.

His failure, to date, had probably come through the very group he had founded, the Libertà. If not the entire group, it was assumed that at least one of its members, Nicolo Palmori—one of Amani's lieutenants—had betrayed the leader.

When Amani was arrested for murder, the supplying of arms to known terrorists, and treason, his enemies within the group—led by Palmori—took over what was left of Amani's fortune and the group.

Amani himself was incarcerated in the maximum security prison at Castel Montferrato for a term of twenty-five years.

It was now the eighth year of his sentence, and his former group—under the leadership of Nicolo Palmori—was in disarray.

"It's our hunch," Hawk continued, "that if Amani were out of prison, it would be *he*—and not Palmori—who would be the Libertà's representative at the KGB's little party."

Carter had groaned inwardly but kept his face an expressionless mask. He could already see what was coming.

"And, Nick, if you gained Amani's confidence by being the one to break him out of jail, you might also be elected to accompany him as, shall we say, his protector."

"Why would he need a protector?"

Hawk averted his eyes, suddenly becoming very interested in a painting on the far office wall. "Well," he said at last, "obviously, when Amani is free, Palmori's people will go after him. Also, since Amani didn't always agree with the Russians when he was in power, it can be supposed that they, too, would like to discourage his attendance."

Carter felt his hackles come up, and he let them.

"You mean I've got to bust this guy out of a jail without letting him know I'm a plant, then keep both the KGB and his own people off his ass until I can get him to a place God-knows-where for a meeting God-knows-when?"

"Exactly. It's right up your alley, Nick. Now, we do have a plan. There is a woman in Manhattan named Naomi Bartinelli . . ."

Carter finished his drink and chuckled as he set the glass back on the tray before him.

"Something amusing?" Carlotta asked, pulling the earphones away and flipping the switch on the control console in the armrest.

"Just going over the whole thing in my head."

"And it's funny?"

"Deliriously," he replied. "I've decided that we've got about a ten percent chance of coming out alive."

They landed at Amsterdam's Schiphol airport at eleven-ten. Customs were cleared quickly, and by noon they were in a Mercedes taxi heading for 1 Professor Tulpplein.

They mounted the steps to the imposing stone structure of the Amstel and moved into its sweeping, three-story-high main lobby.

"I have a reservation. Two rooms adjoining. Kashmir."

"Yes, sir."

Both rooms were luxurious and high up with a view of the whole city.

"We won't be able to do much until this evening," Carter said. "Tired?"

Carlotta shrugged. "More uneasy than tired."

Carter brushed his lips across her forehead and lightly caressed her cheeks with his hands. "I'll call Garrett. It's likely he has the contact for our meet set up by now. Why don't you freshen up and try to rest for a while? We can have an early dinner."

Carlotta nodded and moved toward the connecting door. Just before she closed it behind her, Carter thought he caught a look in her eye.

He dismissed it as the lock clicked, and he headed for the lobby and a pay phone.

"It will take about twenty minutes, sir," the overseas operator said in barely accented English. "If you will leave your name at your hotel desk, I will have you paged."

Carter grabbed a quick sandwich and was just sipping the last of his coffee when the page came.

"This is Kashmir."

"Yes, sir. I am ready with your call. Go ahead, New York."

Both men waited for the distinctive click of the operator departing the line, and then Carter spoke.

"It's me. Are you on, Al?"

"Oh, yeah. Everything is set. Our lady in Manhattan is a very efficient conduit."

"And the computer codes were no problem?"

"None. Child's play for an old-time genius like me."

Carter grinned. "I love your modesty. Give it to me."

"All right. You are Jasmine. Your contact is Oakhurst. The contact will be confirmed with the word 'decibel.' Use it in a sentence."

"Got it," Carter replied. "When?"

"Tonight. Take a boat ride on the Singel Canal at nine o'clock; it's the number three boat. Get off at Kroman. Two blocks down from the canal, there is a café called The Jazzman. Your contact will pick you up there. It will be a woman.''

"Anything else?''

"Maybe,'' Al said and floated from the phone for a moment. When he returned, Carter could hear papers rattling. ''I've uncovered a couple of earlier deals where Kashmir has used Oakhurst. It might be good for you to know about them, as further proof of who you are.''

"Good man, Al.''

Garrett quickly ran through the details of the previous two arms deals, and Carter catalogued them in his mind.

"That's it. I don't imagine I'll be hearing from you again.''

"I don't like the way you say that, Al,'' Carter said with a chuckle. "I owe you a dinner in Arlington in six weeks. I'll be there to pay off.''

"You're on.''

"Ciao.''

Carter returned to his room, stripped, and took a long shower. When he emerged from the bath with a towel around his middle, the door linking his room to Carlotta's was ajar.

She was in bed, with just the sheet over her long, slim body. Her eyes were open, and they rolled his way when he stepped into the doorway.

"Are we on?''

Carter nodded. "Tonight. I'll give you the details over dinner. Can't you sleep?''

"I told you, I'm more uneasy than tired.''

The look was age-old, and Carter didn't miss it. He moved to the side of the bed and stood looking down at her. The drapes were pulled, the only light coming from his own room through the open door behind him.

He leaned forward, hooked a thumb in the sheet at the top

of her breasts, and slowly pushed it down to her knees.

She was naked.

Only her arm moved as she tugged the towel from his body.

Her eyes roamed with approval over his body. His chest was a solid plate of muscle, and his belly was like a washboard. Thick ropes of muscle rippled down from his shoulders through his arms, and he moved into the bed beside her.

Without a word she moved to him, kissing his chest, her lips heating the flesh while her hands worked to excite him.

"Do you think this is wise?" Carter asked.

"No, but I don't give a damn. Do you?"

"No."

Her face was close to his. He loosened the coils of her hair, and it cascaded down around her shoulders like a black waterfall. She twisted her head from side to side, whipping his face with the silken strands.

"Sadist," he teased.

"Masochist," she replied. "I'm prolonging the agony."

"Then let's get down to it."

His hands reached behind her to fill with the lush swells of her buttocks. He then pulled her forward until his lips could find the tips of her throbbing breasts.

Carlotta curled her fingers in his hair, pressed his face tighter against her for a second, then pulled his head back.

"I love that."

"Then why stop?"

"Because I want more."

Again her head moved, and her hair whipped the length of his body, missing not one square inch of skin.

Carter was not passive through all this. His hands stroked the silken length of her back, squeezed her buttocks, and rolled and molded her breasts that hung away from her body when she bent over.

"Enough," he finally growled, tugging her up and over him.

She pressed herself against him, her breasts spreading as they flattened to his chest. He kissed her wildly, then pulled back and rolled her over.

He took her in one smashing second, and the room began to spin around them. His lips muffled her cries as he drove himself against her.

His body fit hers perfectly as his hands found her breasts. Each time he crashed against her, Carlotta's body moved an inch or two on the smooth surface of the sheet.

"Do it . . . do it!" she suddenly cried.

He did, all of it, until she arched toward him, urging him with every gesture and sound.

Slowly, and together, in matching rhythms they moved, each sensing the tide of rising passion in the other until their bodies were whirlpools of frenzied motion.

Suddenly, with her nails digging into his straining back, she arched and writhed as though her entire body had become a taut cord about to snap.

And then it did, and Carter with her.

Both their bodies settled with slowly diminishing spasms until Carter rolled to her side. She snuggled against him, molding the length of her body tightly to him.

"What time do you leave?" she asked, all desire drained now from her voice.

"Around nine."

"It will be nonstop from there, won't it?"

"Yes," he said, and nodded.

"Good luck," she whispered.

She relaxed against him, and just before sleep came, he felt her tug his hand upward to cover the pouting firmness of her breast.

The Jazzman was filled with hippies ranging in age from late teens to early forties. A pungent, acrid odor hung in the air, and the tables were filled with wine bottles.

It was obvious why the little café had been chosen; Carter stuck out like a sore thumb. He guessed that whoever his contact was, she would also be ''different'' from the crowd.

Just inside the door, something resembling Vampira sat at a small table with an open cigar box in front of her.

Carter dropped a few bills into the box, moved on into the club, and found what looked to be the last empty table.

On the stage sat a gorilla with the face of a cherub, dangling a banjo in his paws. He wore greasy motorcycle boots, faded and patched blue jeans, and a wrinkled blue work shirt.

Mournful and unintelligible sounds came from between his lips as he listlessly strummed the banjo.

A lean blonde moved toward Carter. Her feet were bare, and her hair was a tawny tangle to her shoulders. She looked to be about sixteen.

''Wine?''

''Scotch,'' Carter replied.

''We have only wine.''

''I'll have wine . . . two glasses.''

She disappeared with a sharp little wiggle and was back in less than a minute. She plopped the bottle on the table and shifted her weight to one hip.

''You want hashish too?''

Carter's nose wrinkled. Now he recognized the smell that had assaulted his nostrils when he had entered the club. Hashish was common, and legal, in Amsterdam.

"No."

"Five florin," she said, holding out her hand.

He gave her a five-florin note and some coins. She ambled away, and Carter poured a glass of the wine. It was awful, but at least he didn't grimace.

Carter didn't have long to wait. The mournful singer was just stepping down for a hash break when she came through the door. One roll around the room with her eyes and he was spotted.

She was short and compact beneath a big poncho and a pair of snug jeans. Her face was stark white, devoid of makeup, and her eyes were almost concealed beneath dark bangs.

Carter thought that she would have fit right into the place if it hadn't been for her hands. They always tell the story, and these hands said the short creature in the poncho would never see forty again.

"May I join you?"

"Please do."

She sat as he poured wine into the second glass.

"Are you a tourist in Amsterdam?"

Carter shook his head. "I have business with a Mr. Oakhurst."

"And what are you called?"

"Jasmine."

The slight tenseness left the hand and arm holding the glass. She set it on the table and leaned forward. "And . . . ?"

"And the decibel level of chatter in this place is deafening. Could we go somewhere else?"

"One moment."

And then she was gone, into the darkness beyond the rear door of the café.

Carter guessed that somewhere back there was a telephone. He lit a cigarette and waited.

She was back in less than two minutes. "Mr. Oakhurst is nearby."

Carter took her elbow to guide her through the crowd. He almost missed it, a quick but deft exchange between the woman and two of the rowdier men at the bar. Just as they passed, arm in arm, into the street, Carter saw the two men separate themselves from the rest of the crowd.

They were silent for two blocks before Carter spoke out of the side of his mouth. "We're being followed."

"I know. They belong to us."

"Trusting, aren't you?"

"No," she said, and smiled. "It is a very dangerous business. You, of all people, should know that."

At the canal, they turned and followed it for another few blocks. Suddenly she grasped his arm and halted.

"There, the fourth floor. Knock twice, wait, and knock twice again."

It was an old house of crumbling red brick turning gray from years. She made sure he understood which one, then faded from his side into the shadows.

Slowly, he ambled toward the entrance and climbed the steps. The front door opened into a small alcove. Beyond the second door was a hall and rotting stairs.

Carter covered the four flights of stairs three at a time and rapped sharply on the floor's only door. He waited ten seconds, then rapped again. An ear to the thin panel told him that someone was very carefully twisting the lock on the other side.

"Yes?" came a thin, reedy voice through a crack in the door.

"My name is Jasmine. I've come to see Mr. Oakhurst."

"Come in."

Carter stepped through the crack into pitch darkness.

"Stand right there, please."

The voice was behind him. The hands that patted him down came from in front.

"He is not armed."

The door closed behind him, and a bare bulb blinked on in the ceiling. The room was ratty, a table, a few chairs, and a cot its only furnishings.

The man before Carter was short and squat. His face was lined, and his skin was puckered beneath his neck as if he had once been much heavier but had shriveled. A Walther PPK was lolling easily in his right hand.

"You are Oakhurst?" Carter asked.

"I am Oakhurst."

Carter turned slowly.

He was tall and scarecrow thin. His face beneath a heavy growth of beard was gaunt, the cheeks hollow, the eyes sunken in dark pockets.

He looks strung out, Carter thought, *or tubercular*.

Carter knew it was the latter when the man moved to the table and immediately started hacking into a ready handkerchief he held in his right hand.

"I trust our last two exchanges met with your approval?" he managed to say between coughing spasms.

"Quite," Carter said, slipping into an opposite chair. The squat man, still playing with the Walther, moved to a window ledge and sat. "Except, of course, the vests on the first shipment were not of the quality you said, and you shorted me two crates of mortar shells on the second."

The man's thin lips creased into a smile, and Carter sighed inwardly, giving silent thanks to Garrett's analytical thinking.

"My apologies. I will make it up to you with a credit on these items."

He flattened a piece of paper and a map on the table.

"Now, shall we get down to business? The goods are

currently in a warehouse in The Hague. They are still legit, with an end-use certificate for Caracas. We can ship by air or by sea, depending on your true destination.''

Carter flipped the map around and traced his finger down the coast of Italy. ''Here.''

The man's eyes darted down and then back up to meet Carter's. Beneath his beard, the jawline tensed as his teeth clenched. ''We can't consign at that distance and you know it.''

''You will this time,'' Carter replied in a flat, even voice. The squat man lifted his butt from the windowsill and steadied the Walther. ''And tell your man to put that away or I will give him an enema with it.''

The man took one step forward, and Oakhurst held up his hand. ''I shall have to make a call. One moment.''

He stood and moved through a curtain serving as a door into another room. Carter lit a cigarette and turned to the other man.

''Sit down.''

He did, and slid the Walther into his belt.

It took almost a half hour before the bearded man returned to his chair.

''It can be done. A Libyan freighter, the *Alamein*, departs Marseille in two days' time. We will recrate there and ship as pottery.''

''Can the exchange be made at sea?''

The man nodded and jotted on a pad. ''These coordinates in five days. Midnight . . . sharp.''

Carter memorized the coordinates and touched his lighter to the paper. When it was ashes, he stood.

''Now, the money.''

Carter opened his shirt. From beneath it he withdrew a fat money belt and draped it across the table.

''There is fifty thousand. The remainder when the exchange is made and I have all the goods.''

"Agreed," the man replied, but the crooked smile beneath the beard told Carter the truth.

He had just made a cardinal error in the purchase of munitions from an illegal arms dealer. Oakhurst had fifty thousand, and he still had the cargo.

Ergo, he could run with the down payment and sell the arms to the next bidder.

It was unethical but very practical.

A man like the bearded one before him wouldn't worry about losing a good customer like Jasmine. There were too many other good customers right around the corner, and fifty thousand was a good night's work if one didn't have to deliver anything for it.

But Carter had made this cardinal error on purpose. If there was one thing a man like Oakhurst feared more than making a bad deal, it was death itself. He would go to any lengths to protect his own skin, even to the point of remaining honest. He simply had to be shown the way.

Carter meant to do just that.

"By the way, give me the number here—in case there is a change of plans after I make my delivery contact tonight.''

The two men exchanged wary glances, and then the bearded one seemed to shrug with his eyes.

Carter could almost read his thoughts: *Why not give the number to this fool? He'll never live long enough to dial it!*

He clipped it off between thin lips, and Carter left the room.

On the street, Carter paused to light a cigarette, the corner of his eye on the fourth-floor window. When the light went off and on twice, he moved off at a steady, brisk pace.

FIVE

It was cat and mouse for almost fifteen minutes. Carter never saw them behind him, but he heard their heels matching his pace as he moved farther and farther into the old part of the city.

The streets had long since given themselves up to narrow alleys, and streetlights were nonexistent. The only illumination came from an occasional barred window high in the walls through which he passed.

As he searched for just the right place, Carter made no effort to elude them. On purpose, his own heels left a clearly audible trail that only a deaf person wouldn't be able to follow.

And then he saw it, a tiny alley. It was no more than a corridor between low buildings.

He turned into it and immediately broke into a run. They were still behind him, making the turn themselves, as Carter veered between the buildings. As he sprinted, he paused at every alcove to try the doors he found.

Behind him, he could hear two sets of pounding feet. He wondered how close behind them the woman would be.

Carter was about to halt and try the game where he was,

when the alley before him swerved in a Y to the left and right. He chose the left and, around the corner, checked his flight with a growl of satisfaction.

The alley ended with a heavy, iron-studded double door. The entry was slightly ajar, and a bare bulb cast eerie yellow light through the crack between door and jamb.

It was perfect.

Behind him, the footsteps slowed in caution. They thought they had Carter boxed, and now, hopefully, they would move in for the kill.

Carter darted through the opening and left the heavy door open a crack behind him.

It was a large wine cellar, fitted with long rows of racks on which rested many hundreds of dusty bottles under a whitewashed stone roof. He darted along the wall, glancing hurriedly down each row. Each ended in a blank stone wall . . . except the last. At the far end of that was a small vaulted door.

Carter checked it and smiled in satisfaction when he found it locked.

There was no other way out.

Now, Carter thought, settling into a crouch behind one of the high wine racks, *the hunted becomes the hunter*.

A tenseness in the muscle of his right forearm released the spring in Hugo's sheath, sending the deadly stiletto sliding forward into his hand.

There was a deathly silence, and then the faint creak of the entrance door opening. Without hesitation, Carter clutched a half bottle of wine from one of the racks and threw it unerringly at the bulb.

There was a popping sound as the light went, and then a louder crash as the bottle shattered on the stone floor. This was quickly followed by guttural curses and the sound of falling bodies as the two of them rolled into the room. Then Carter heard the dull thud of the door closing behind them.

He's not armed, the squat man had said after patting Carter down.

Hopefully, he had relayed this information to the two outside men and the woman.

Now the cellar was completely dark. Clutching the stiletto in his hand, Carter crouched in a corner and reasoned his next move. There were two of them, and they might be joined shortly by a third, the woman.

They would probably use knives, but Carter guessed they would have guns as well. He could only hope that they, like himself, wanted to keep this thing private. If so, guns wouldn't be a factor.

Since there were only two of them, they couldn't search the passages between the rows of wine racks one by one and be sure that he hadn't slipped by at the unguarded end.

Carter guessed that one would start by feeling his way carefully around the perimeter walls, either to drive him toward the other one who would be waiting for him, or to make Carter move and perhaps betray his whereabouts by some slight noise.

If Carter was guessing correctly, what was the best maneuver to counter it?

His only hope was to get at one of them first and hope the other would go for the sound in the confusion.

The problem was, which way to go? He didn't know which way around the outer walls they would be moving.

Still crouching, he listened intently. There were no footfalls, but then, if they were moving, it was probably on their hands and knees.

Then he thought he heard a faint clink, as though one bottle had been touched against another. It seemed to have come from the far end of the right-hand wall leading away from his corner.

Still in a half crouch, his toes barely making a whisper on the stone floor, Carter moved to his right. As he came to the corner at the far end of the wall along which he was moving, he stopped to listen once more. He was sure that the wall he had now reached was the one that led to the entrance door.

He thought of making a noise and drawing them in, when he heard the breathing, almost beside him.

With the greatest care, Carter groped for the end of the nearest wine rack and eased himself across the space and into the passage between that rack and the next. In spite of the exertion, he managed first to hold his breath, and then to breathe cautiously and silently.

What he could not decide was whether, a moment or two earlier, his own breathing had been as apparent to the man as his had been to Carter.

The breathing could no longer be heard. He dug in the pocket of his slacks until his fingers found a book of matches. Carefully, he tucked the flap under the matches and folded two of them down. Holding the match heads in place with his thumb over the striking surface, he concentrated hard, trying to discern the slightest indication of where his prey was.

And then he heard it: the barely perceptible scrape of a toe or the leather sole of a shoe against the stone. It came from the wall directly opposite him.

Tensing his whole body, Carter scraped the matches over the striking surface.

They had fooled him. One was directly in front of him, staring at the flaring matches in Carter's left hand in surprise. But the other one wasn't across the room as Carter had thought. He was in the next aisle over, and already moving around toward him.

But now Carter only had time for the one in front of him as the man lunged. Carter thrust forward with his left hand, smashing the burning matches into the man's face. His right hand, holding the stiletto, flashed up from the floor.

There was a scream of pain as the matches seared the man's face, but it became a dry rattle as the stiletto found a home in his throat. It was dark again, but Carter knew the man was done when he felt warm blood run across his hand.

Number one dropped like a stone, and just as he hit, the second one struck a clubbing blow across Carter's back. It sent Carter reeling against the wall. He hit, whirled, and swung his left arm.

It was a lucky blow. The heel of his hand struck number two full in the face. He could feel cartilage, bone, and muscle all turn to gel. Then the man was sliding down his body, trying to hold on as Carter tried just as hard to twist free.

Somehow he managed to seize an ankle and pull. Carter's feet went out from under him, and as he went down, Hugo came out of his hand. He heard it hit the floor and slither off somewhere under the bottles. In an instant, the whole weight of the other man's body fell on Carter, knocking the breath from him and pinning him down.

Just as quickly, Carter felt himself being flipped. A hand slid across his face, and the inner side of an elbow sought his throat.

The intent was all too clear. The man was going to bend Carter's head back until the spine snapped.

Carter tensed his throat muscles before the grip became stationary. At the same time, he managed to get his chin slightly under the man's wrist.

It wasn't much for leverage, but it was enough to sink his teeth deeply into the flesh.

He bit down with all the strength in his jaws, bringing a

howl of pain from the man's throat. Carter waited until he could taste blood and feel bone with his teeth, and then he started grinding.

It worked.

The arm loosened from his throat. Carter bucked upward, raising the straddling body off him. Before the man could come back down again, Carter slipped over and brought both knees up in a crunching blow to the other's groin.

There was another howl of pain, and the man fell forward limply. Carter brought his left forearm across the windpipe, folded his right arm around the neck, and pressured it in a vise.

Even in unconsciousness the man struggled, but only for a few seconds. Then he settled down against Carter again.

Carter was about to push the very dead weight off him, when there was a scraping sound and a sudden shaft of light.

From where he lay, pressed against the floor, Carter could see beneath the bottles ranged on the wine racks. At the far corner of the room, where the vaulted door had been locked, there was now bright light slanting across the stone floor.

He could see two pairs of boots. The object being lowered to the floor between them he guessed to be a wine litter. Evidently, two servants had entered through the small door from the kitchens above to fill an order for wine.

"The damn light is off again."

"Did you bring a flashlight?"

"Of course not."

"Open the door a little wider. Maybe that will be enough light."

The boots moved around the racks, coming toward the aisle in which Carter lay with a body beside him and another half on top of him.

He tensed, ready to heave the corpse and run, when they turned one aisle short and moved down it.

They moved down the aisle, gathering bottles as they

came. Not daring to breathe, Carter followed the progress of the two pair of boots in the slanting yellow light.

And then his eye caught a glint of light off metal on the floor. Directly in front of the first pair of boots lay his stiletto. Four, perhaps even three more steps, and one of the boots would kick it or step on it.

Using every bit of strength in his body, still partially holding the corpse over him lest something in the man's pockets clatter if he were dumped off, Carter wriggled to the side. Inch by inch, he approached the wine rack.

The boots were shuffling sideways now, accompanied by the clink of bottles going into the litter.

The boot was six inches from the stiletto when Carter slid his hand under the lowest rack.

His fingertips matched the distance of the servant's boot from the knife: two inches.

He wriggled again. The body was slipping off. The boots were sliding.

There was a crash.

"You idiot! What happened?" His boot kicked the stiletto right into Carter's hand, but the sound of the crashing bottle had distracted him.

"It's too damned dark. Let's get out of here before we break more."

"What about this mess?"

"Clean it up tomorrow."

Carter slid the knife back to his side of the rack and held his breath until the door closed behind them. The moment he heard the bolt slide, he pushed the body away and sprinted to the outside door.

One quick glance through the crack in the door told him the immediate area outside was deserted.

But that could be—and probably was—misleading. There was still the woman.

He darted into the alley and paused. From a narrow shaft of

light coming down from an upper window, he assessed the damage.

It wasn't good.

Physically he was all right, but he looked as though he had just barely survived World War III.

There was a rent in the side of his coat, and one sleeve hung half off. Another tear in his shirt revealed an ugly red welt. Beneath it, everything he wore was splotched with blood.

It would be back alleys all the way back to the hotel. But only after a short detour.

Somewhere near the mouth of the curving alley between the buildings in front of him, Carter knew she would be waiting.

Quickly, he unlaced his shoes and retied them to the back of his belt under his jacket. Then he moved forward in a low, running crouch, keeping himself almost entirely in the shadows.

He moved around the curve without a pause, and then around a second.

Just around it, Carter saw her, dead ahead, about twenty feet away. In each hand was a shoe with the heel removed. In place of the heel on each shoe there was a two-sided, six-inch dagger.

"Amal . . . ?"

Carter didn't answer her, and he didn't slacken his speed. She was partially illuminated by a pool of light from a nearby house. When he charged into the same light, she recognized him and bent into a fighting stance.

Carter didn't change direction, pause, or reverse. He just barreled ahead. Three feet from her, she feinted to the left. Instead of countering and trying to escape around her, Carter moved with her.

It took her by surprise, but she gamely tried to nail him before he hit.

It didn't work.

Carter grabbed her wrists and turned them as they collided. The knives bit deep, one in the fleshy part of each shoulder.

She muffled her own cry of pain as she went down, and Carter ran on over her.

At the mouth of the alley he looked back once, and saw the mask of torment and pain on her face as she pulled first one and then the second piece of steel from her own body.

He hit the larger street, went a block, and then darted into a doorway. He waited, crouched, controlling his breathing. When ten minutes had elapsed, he chanced a look.

Nothing.

Slowly, still in his stocking feet, he retraced his steps and looked down into the narrow alley.

She was gone.

It took him another two minutes to find a spot of blood on the sidewalk, and then another.

He followed the spots for seven blocks, until he was sure of her destination, and then he broke off and headed for the hotel.

Two blocks short of the Amstel, on an dimly lit street, he darted into a phone booth and dialed the number the arms dealer had given him.

The woman had less distance to travel than Carter had to the hotel. It was a good bet that she had already arrived.

The phone was answered on the fifth ring.

"Oakhurst, this is Jasmine."

"Yes." The voice was noncommittal.

"Did you receive my message?"

"Yes." Now it was a whisper.

"Is she alive?"

"Barely."

"Too bad. The other two are in a wine cellar . . . dead. You'd better find out from her where, before they are found.

Are you listening?''

"Yes."

"I only let this sort of thing happen once, Oakhurst. I have a long arm. If it happens again, you're out of business . . . permanently. Do you understand?''

"I do.''

"Then I shall expect our rendezvous to take place with all the goods intact. That will happen, won't it, Oakhurst?''

"It will happen, Jasmine. You have my word on it.''

"Your word to me is like your life . . . shit. Just remember that.''

Carter hung up and trotted the two remaining blocks to the hotel. He went all the way around to the loading dock and entered there. Between the kitchen and his floor he ran into only one person, a drunk who looked worse than Carter, vainly trying to find a hole for his key.

Carter went on through his own room and into Carlotta's. It was empty, but the bathroom light was on.

She had one foot on the floor and the other raised, about to step into a nightgown.

"Beautiful,'' Carter whispered.

The foot dropped and the gown came up to cover her naked body.

When she realized who it was, she released her breath with a whooshing sound and carelessly dropped the gown back to the floor.

"My God, what happened to you?''

"You should see the other guys.''

He moved around her and turned on the shower.

"Well?''

"It's a go,'' he said, adjusting the taps. "A Libyan freighter will be off the coast of Italy in five days' time. I'll rendezvous, and we'll set up an off-load point on shore.''

"Then I should call Palmori tonight.''

Carter nodded. "And I'll call the airport and get you a morning flight to Rome. But in the meantime . . ."

Effortlessly he lifted her and stepped into the tub.

"Nick . . . your suit . . ."

"It's ruined anyway," he said lightly. "Now, about tonight . . ."

SIX

Carter flew to Nice via Paris after making sure, through a few well-placed bribes on the docks, that the crates of ''pottery'' had been loaded aboard the freighter *Alamein*. From Nice, he trained through Monaco and across the Italian frontier into San Remo.

Dressed unobtrusively as a camera-toting American tourist on a slim budget, he checked into a small pension in the hills high above the beach. He didn't unpack his small bag, since he would only be using the room for a few hours.

After a quick nap, he changed into a blue denim jacket, jeans, and a workman's shirt, and left the pension. The sky had darkened, and a light, drizzling rain had forced shoppers from the streets and bathers from the beaches.

At the post office, he slipped the Kashmir passport through the cage and got back two letters. Both had been mailed in Rome two days before.

The first was from Carlotta, with a key:

Rendezvous Torta, 5:00 set.
Eight: three lookouts, five handlers.
Funds set as per prearrangement.
Palmori not suspicious but will not attend.

Inside the second envelope, he found a note that was even more terse:

Guido's on Via Colonna. 3:00

Carter checked his watch. It was already a little past the hour. But it wouldn't matter; Santoni would wait.

He knew only the larger avenues of the small resort village, but a single inquiry of a passerby led him easily to Via Colonna.

Guido's was a good-size sidewalk café with about twenty tables outside and more of the same inside. There were a few drinkers and diners under the exterior awning, but none of them even glanced up at Carter.

He stepped through the door and squinted his eyes against the gloom. The tables and booths were covered with checkered cloths, and in the center of each, the ever present wine bottle with its hardened wax drippings and a cheap candle stuck in the neck.

Carter spotted his man in the darkness of a corner booth. The two men nodded, and Carter moved through the tables.

"You are late."

"I missed my first train out of Nice."

"Sit."

Tony Santoni was a small, compact man of about forty. He had wavy black hair, a pale face for a native of southern Italy, and intelligent eyes.

For years he had been registered as a master captain on anything that sailed from 165 feet on down.

Sailing was his passion.

So was antiterrorism.

Tony Santoni was a major in Italy's SID, and for the last ten years he had been one of the government agency's best undercover men.

Carter had already worked with the man on more than one rumble, and he trusted him completely.

Two glasses had already been filled from a large carafe of wine. Santoni pushed one toward Carter and smiled.

"You look fit," he said. "Don't you ever age?"

"In our business, Tony, one never ages. We just up and die one day."

"How true. *Salute!*"

The two men drank and then leaned forward, their eyes riveted over the wineglasses.

"You have the boat?"

The Italian nodded. "A forty-foot Corsair with enclosed cabin and twin Cummins. It will do over sixty knots in a calm sea, and it is already rigged for arms."

"Smuggling boat?"

"What else? We liberated it from a bunch of Turks in the Adriatic about two months ago."

"Is it ready to roll?"

"Absolutely, complete with spare tanks. How far do we have to go?"

Carter fished a piece of paper from the denim jacket and spread it between them.

"We rendezvous with the freighter here, just to the northwest of Corsica, at midnight."

Santoni scratched his stubbled chin with the rim of the wineglass. "We had best leave right after nightfall. Even then we will have to push it."

"But we can make it?"

"Yes. Where do we deliver?"

"A fishing village called Torta, here, between Cecina and Livorno."

"I know it."

"Figuring a half hour for the unloading, can we make it by five o'clock in the morning?"

"You can bet on it," Santoni said with a wide smile. "This little bambino will fairly fly."

"What if this storm gets worse?"

"It won't. It is already moving north. An hour out and we will probably have calm seas."

"Good. Do we need any crew?"

"Not if you are as good a sailor as you used to be."

Carter grinned. "I think I am." He folded the paper and tucked it into the other man's jacket. "I'll pick up our treasurer as soon as I leave here. Where do I meet you?"

"There is a cove just this side of the frontier. You know Ristorante Roma, on the coast highway?"

"I know it."

"It is just east of there. As close after dark as possible."

Carter squeezed the other man's wrist and slid from the booth. "I left Kashmir's things and the papers in the Pension Garibaldi, up on the hill."

"I'll inform the locals that it is our business."

"And there will be eight of them, three probably on the perimeters and well armed."

"I'll tell our people down there to take them out first."

"*Ciao,*" Carter said with a nod and strolled from the café.

Carter took the coast road and walked nearly a mile before turning up a narrow path into the hills. The rain had picked up, and a few thunderclouds had moved in.

He almost missed the smaller hut among the rocks and would have if he hadn't seen the smoke curling up into the sky.

The door was in two parts, with a tiny, glazed pane at eye level. The latch wouldn't give, so he tried the key.

It was one large, sparsely furnished room with an open kitchen in the rear and a small hallway to his right. He was halfway toward the hallway when a young woman stepped from it into the room.

She had a round, intense face, a deep olive complexion, and black hair that hung wetly down below her shoulders.

When she saw Carter, she stopped abruptly, the towel in her hands halfway to her hair. If possible, her youthful features hardened even more.

"Who are you?"

"Who the hell are *you?*"

She started edging back toward the hallway. The sash that held her lightweight housecoat together loosened slightly, revealing a lot of her shapely figure and heavy breasts that didn't fit her little-girl face.

"If you'll notice," Carter said, "I let myself in with a key."

He extended his left hand, palm up, with the key in its center. That stopped her movement, and some of the animal tenseness seemed to fade from her eyes and body.

She reached for the key, but just before her fingers touched it, Carter tilted his hand away. When she grabbed for it, he grabbed her, locking both of her wrists in a steely grip with his left hand. At the same time, he squeezed Hugo into his right hand and brought the tip of the stiletto up against her throat as he slammed her against the wall.

"Don't play twenty questions with me, little girl. I'm supposed to meet a man here. Where is he?"

"I . . . I'm the only one here."

"Then who are you?"

"Palmori. I am Sophia Palmori."

Carter dropped her and resheathed Hugo. "You should have said so. Nicolo's daughter?"

"Yes. I was frightened. You are Ali Kashmir?"

Carter nodded. "Why you?"

"There has been a great deal of internal strife within our organization. I was the only one my father could trust with such a great amount of money."

She tightened the housecoat around her and stepped back. Her eyes, as the panic and fear faded from them, were already hardening up again.

"How old are you?"

"Eighteen," she replied, jutting her chin forward defiantly. "But I am a seasoned soldier. I have been fighting our cause against the warmongers and imperialists since I was twelve."

Christ, Carter thought. *Sick, sick, sick.*

"Where is it?"

"The money?"

"What else? That's all I'm interested in." She hesitated, her full lower lip floating between her even, white teeth. "No money, no deal. I'm not moving from San Remo until I lay eyes on it."

She moved down the narrow hall, Carter right behind her. From behind two loose boards in the rear of a closet, she withdrew a leather briefcase. On the bed, she flipped the catches and lifted the lid.

"Swiss francs and dollars."

They were in neat stacks, large bills still bound in bank wrappers.

Carter selected two of them at random and ruffled them beside his ear.

"Don't you want to count it?"

"I already have," he replied. "Lock it back up. Do you have anything to eat in this place?"

Carter moved down the narrow, almost invisible steps that had been cut by hand into the side of the cliff. Far above them and to the side, the lights of Ristorante Roma blinked against the clear night sky.

True to Tony Santoni's weather report, the storm had about blown itself out and was now headed on north toward France.

The girl, dressed in a dark sweater, blue jeans, and sneakers, trailed right at his heels.

"Hold it."

He stopped so abruptly she nearly crashed into his backside. They were only a few feet from the water, with a pale moon glinting off its surface but revealing nothing of the shoreline except black, jutting rocks.

Carter flipped the switch on his penlight twice, then motioned the girl forward.

"What was that for?"

"To let my man know we're coming. He doesn't like to be surprised."

They dipped into a deep hollow, and there, completely hidden from the sea and the cliffs, was the long, sleek Corsair gently bobbing against a makeshift pier.

Lounging against its gleaming rails was Tony Santoni, a Uzi submachine gun cradled in his arms like a sleeping baby.

"This is Tony. Tony, Sophia Palmori."

"A girl?"

"A woman, bastard," she hissed.

Santoni smiled, his eyes sweeping her front where her breasts seemed ready to burst through the sweater.

"Not much doubt of that," he quipped. "Come aboard!"

Santoni cast off the bow and aft lines as Carter and Sophia moved into the wheelhouse.

"This is beautiful," she gasped. "Do you own this?"

"We lease . . . very short-term. Through that hatch is the main cabin. Somewhere down there is a bar. Fix yourself something and open a beer for me. I'll be down in a minute."

From the scowl on her face Carter knew she didn't like taking orders, but she went, banging the briefcase on the hatchway as she went through.

He cranked up the dual Cummins diesels and felt a ripple pass over his skin as the power plant's low, guttural roar vibrated through the boat. He adjusted the twin throttles to idle and snapped on a portable radar that had been mounted on the dash just beneath the windshield.

The set hummed, the screen flashed white, and then it settled down to its normal green color with the yellow circling wand.

Santoni crawled over the low bulkhead and dropped to the wheelhouse deck.

"All lines clear?" Carter asked.

"All clear."

The big boat responded like a finely turned race car as Carter pushed the throttles forward and the bow lifted. In no time they were beyond the bay doing a little over forty knots, and Carter was setting the course as Santoni called out the coordinates.

"Take it!" Carter said over the roaring engines.

He moved from the wheel, and the Italian took his place. They skimmed the water for about a mile before Santoni lit a cigarette and threw a sideways glance at Carter.

"Why did old man Palmori send her?"

Carter shrugged. "Didn't trust anybody else, I guess."

"Or didn't trust you . . . or Carlotta."

"Why do you say that?"

"Because I know him," Santoni replied. "Sophia's file is as thick as her father's. She is the best he has."

"How so?"

"Five kills that we know about, two of them on the streets of Rome in broad daylight."

"That's sick."

"Sure it's sick, but they are all sick. It is part of the game
. . . brainwash them right from the cradle. Watch yourself,
Nick."

"I will."

Carter went below. An open beer was resting in a roll-
cradle on the bar. The girl was behind it, a glass of wine in her
hand, staring out the porthole.

The moon bathed her features in soft light and dark tones.
It was the first time he had noticed that, in a hard way, she
was quite beautiful.

"Where's the key?" Carter asked, taking a long swallow
from the beer.

"What for?"

"So I can divide up the money . . . their price, and my
commission."

Haughtily, Sophia slid the key across the bar. "You are a
privateer."

"I sure am," Carter said, opening the briefcase and starting his count.

"We need people like you now," she said softly, "to
supply the revolution. But one day—"

"One day, little girl, we'll all be dead and not one damned
soul will remember who sold or who shot what we buy and
sell."

"Death means nothing to me. I am a revolutionary."

"Good. Because if my supplier tries to cross me again,
we'll probably have a fire fight on our hands before we pull
away from that freighter. Can you use an Uzi?"

"I can handle any gun that has ever been made."

"I'll just bet you can."

And he meant it.

It was in her eyes: the joy of killing. Now he was glad he
had surprised her in the cottage unarmed. If she then had had

the little Beretta he knew now was in the waistband of her jeans, he might have been forced to kill her.

All guts for the cause and very little hard reasoning, he thought, *that's how they're trained.*

Jesus, using his own daughter.

Carter hoped that one day he would cross Palmori before this was all over.

And he had a sneaking hunch that he would.

SEVEN

"I have them on the radar."

Santoni's voice at the hatchway brought Carter into instant wakefulness. He rolled from the bunk and checked his watch as he went up the ladder. It was 11:45.

"Right there, about eight miles to starboard. We should spot them in about five minutes."

Carter found the little clear blip on the radar screen. "I'll mount the twenty on the roof. Sophia . . . ?"

"Yes?"

"Get the other Uzi from below and set up shop in the bow."

This time she nodded and moved without question. Carter narrowed his eyes and watched the blip move slowly toward their position on the grid.

"You're sure it's the *Alamein?*"

"Almost positive," Santoni replied. "There's not much out here tonight, and nothing that big so close to land."

Carter took his word for it and opened a bulkhead chest set against the port rail of the wheelhouse. Fom the chest he hoisted an 8mm Fiat Model 35 heavy machine gun to his shoulder. The Fiat's portable mount had been replaced with special cotter-key interlocks that fit the disguised stationary mounts on the wheelhouse roof.

There were four three-hundred-round, nondisintegrating belts laid out on the floor of the chest. Carter slung only one over his shoulder.

If three hundred rounds from the Fiat and damage from the two Uzis wouldn't squelch any double cross by Oakhurst, then nothing would.

On the roof he matched the runners, slid the bolts home, and snapped the keys into place. He fed four shells through, rammed one home, and left the weapon cocked.

The Fiat was a vintage gun with a lot of drawbacks, but it would more than do for the night's work. Just a look at its ugly snout and trailing ammo belt by the men on the freighter would probably be enough.

"There, on the horizon!"

Carter followed the line of Santoni's arm and saw the tiny dot of the freighter's superstructure growing in the moonlight.

He was just finishing the beamlight's rigging when Sophia came back on deck and passed below him, headed for the bow. She had donned a rain slicker and pulled the hood up until it covered her head and most of her face.

Carter wondered if she was worried about being recognized or if she thought the Uzi in her hands would have more clout if its wielder's sex was unknown.

"Send them a couple of quick ones!" Santoni shouted, idling back on the throttles about ten knots.

Carter blinked the beamlight twice and narrowed his eyes at the freighter. There was no response. He waited a full two minutes, then repeated the signal.

This time there was a two-blink answer, and Carter could detect a slight alteration in course.

Santoni laid forward on the throttles again, and the Corsair leaped forward like a scalded cat.

Five minutes later they slid under the bow on the port side, and the Italian goosed the powerful boat into a 360. He laid up directly under the huge loading doors and idled back to about five knots, matching the freighter's speed.

"Ahoy, *Alamein!*" Carter shouted between cupped hands.

A tall, graying man in a long black greatcoat and a visored cap appeared at the rail. "Aye, we're the *Alamein* out of Marseille."

"And are you Captain Rhinemeyer?"

"I am. And you?"

"Jasmine."

"May I come aboard?"

"You may."

A rope ladder slid out of the loading bay as Carter moved away from the machine gun and dropped into the wheelhouse. Minutes later, the tall captain came down the ladder and joined him.

"You look as if you are expecting trouble."

"We are," Carter intoned, unsmiling. "Your employer and my supplier tried to test me a few nights ago in Amsterdam."

The captain shrugged. "I know none of this. I only deliver and take my commission."

"Below," Carter said, and led the way.

It took Rhinemeyer only ten minutes to count and transfer the money from one briefcase to the other.

He's very practiced at it, Carter thought, leading him back on deck.

"Unload."

The arms of twin cranes rolled out almost before the word

was out of the captain's mouth. Pallets, each holding two crates, were rigged on each of them.

There were twelve crates in all, and the complete operation was accomplished in another twenty minutes.

When the last two pallets were unloaded, the captain stepped up on one of them. He gestured, and without a word he was hauled up.

"I hope you get this done quickly," Santoni muttered. "I'd like Interpol to nail that bastard in Caracas."

"Our fish is much, much bigger than this guy," Carter growled. "Cut back your engines."

Santoni did, and the freighter glided on by.

When it was clear and picking up knots, he whirled the wheel and jammed the throttles.

"Think the added weight will make any difference on our ETA?"

Santoni shook his head. "This baby was built for this kind of hauling."

Carter nodded and went below. He stripped to his shorts and was just crawling into a night suit when Sophia dropped through the hatch. Carter was glad to note that Santoni had lifted the Uzi when she passed him.

"It went well?"

"Yes, it did," he replied. "There's a set of these for you on the bunk. They might be a little big. I thought you would be a man."

"They'll work."

Without turning her back, she pulled the sweater over her head and slipped out of the jeans. She wore no bra, and her panties were transparent and barely there.

Carter took one look and turned away.

Nick Carter stood by Tony Santoni at the wheel. Both wore

night suits with skintight black gloves, and their faces had been darkened with midnight grease.

Sophia Palmori lay flat out on her belly in the bow. Like the men she had darkened her features, and now her black-gloved hands nervously fingered the action on the Uzi.

It was her show from here on. She knew who was waiting, where they were, and what they expected to see and hear.

One of the beamlights from the wheelhouse roof had been remounted on the bow deck right beside her. It had been fitted with an adjustable aperture snood that would take its powerful beam down to a sliver of light less than an inch in diameter.

She had already signaled once and had received a quick flash in response.

That had been from about four miles out. Now, with one of the Cummins diesels shut down, they were making their way in at less than five knots.

At that speed, the bow was doing a lot of pitching and yawing the closer they got to the beach. Though both Carter and Santoni knew the scenario of what had already occurred on the beach—and what was about to occur—they played it by the book, outwardly cautious, following Sophia Palmori's every barked command.

Santoni steered in, jerking and swerving like a slow-moving ruptured hare, sometimes easing back on the throttle and cutting his speed, but never once holding the wheel steady for more than a few seconds.

No words passed between the two men. They had already said everything that needed to be said.

Both Uzis—the one in Carter's hands and the one Sophia now cradled in the bow—held doctored magazines with soft rubber bullets. Santoni had seen to that.

Carter's fast friends—the Luger, Wilhelmina, and the

stiletto, Hugo—were wrapped in an oilskin bag and secreted beneath the bar.

"I'll miss them. Take care of them and make sure I get them back after the break."

"Will do."

Carter's cut was back in Sophia's suitcase. If all went well, it would find its way back to the Libertà.

That, Carter thought, would be good for public relations.

"To the right . . . ten degrees," Sophia said in a hoarse whisper.

Santoni moved the wheel just a touch, and the bow responded.

The bright lights of Livorno to their left, and the smaller and dimmer cluster of Marina di Cecina to their right, were all but obscured now by the coastline.

The needle of the rev counter was barely bobbing now as Sophia flicked the light one last time. The reply was immediate.

"Take it straight in!" she hissed.

"Get ready to drop anchor," Santoni said, fighting to keep the bow against the tide.

Carter clamored to the fantail and hunched down over the anchor release. A few clouds had scudded over what moon there was, inking out even the coastline.

"Now!" Sophia rasped from the bow.

Carter released the anchor just as Santoni killed the single diesel. He felt the claw drag and then catch.

The big boat yawed and then began bobbing lazily around on the anchor chain, its movement dictated by the incoming and outgoing tide.

All was deathly still. But only for a second.

They were good; Carter had to give them credit for that. They had slid out to the boat on a raft completely unseen. The only sound was the rubber tires on the side of the raft gently bumping the boat before they came over the side.

The first one to hit the deck looked like a leftover from the Neanderthal period. He had long dirty hair spilling over the top of his turtleneck and spreading out over his massive shoulders.

He faced Carter with two round, evil little eyes and a flat face.

He grunted something unintelligible and walked toward Carter, holding out an enormous paw.

The Killmaster forced himself to give the hulk a friendly smile and took the paw in a shake.

Sophia was instantly at the man's side, beaming. She kissed his ugly face and introduced him as Wombo something-or-other.

Two more men spilled over the rail after the beast as he eyed the crates.

"The raft will only take three of these at a time." His voice was like sandpaper over steel, and it sounded as though it came from deep in a well. "How many are there?"

"Twelve," Carter replied.

The man's face screwed into an intense mask of concentration. "That means four trips."

Carter was amazed he had figured that out by himself.

Wombo directed the other two to take one of the crates. They struggled with it a few feet, until Santoni and then Carter himself joined them. Finally the four of them managed to muscle it to the rail and rope it down to the remaining two men on the raft.

When they turned, Wombo stood patiently waiting, a crate balanced easily on his shoulder.

"My God," Carter gasped as the giant lowered it, also by himself.

"Wombo is very strong," Sophia said at his shoulder.

"I'd say that, yes," Carter replied, throwing her a sideways glance.

Her eyes were still beaming as she watched the unreal man go for another crate. Beneath the night suit, Carter could swear that he saw her breasts rise and fall with each of the big man's movements.

Now, that, Carter thought, *is a very weird pair!*

Carter rode the raft in and helped unload the first three crates. In the process, he strained his eyes into the darkness around and above him, but he could see no signs of movement.

They were about to push the raft off for the second set of crates, when Carter calmly remarked, "You do have perimeter guards around here somewhere, don't you?"

The giant replied with something that sounded like "Ugh" and pointed to three places in the cliffs.

Carter scanned them quickly and still saw no movement. But he wasn't worried. If Tony Santoni's team was as good as Santoni himself, the three watchmen would have already been taken out.

Trip two was uneventful and smooth. The third set of crates had just been loaded when Sophia started to crawl over the side into the raft.

"Where are you going?" Carter asked.

"Ashore. There are only three crates left."

Carter had to think fast. It was imperative that one person escape the net. Sophia was the logical person. She had to stay on the boat.

"There isn't any room on the raft."

"One of the others can stay."

Carter shrugged. "I'll stay myself."

Wombo and the girl exchanged looks. This arms dealer had his money, and there was still a small fortune in arms left on the boat in the three remaining crates.

"I'll stay," she said, slipping the sling of the Uzi from her shoulder and cradling it in her arms.

Carter smiled to himself and threw a quick look and a nod to Santoni in the wheelhouse. Just as he went over the side, he saw the SID man flip one of the toggle switches on the dash.

The switch would activate the twin bow running lights, but no white beams would go shooting through the night. Instead, there would be a dull purple glow behind the lenses barely perceptible to the human eye.

The SID men on the cliffs would be wearing night goggles. To them, the infrared beams emanating from the bow lights would be bright and clear.

So would their message: "Take them this trip!"

It took the five of them, plus Carter, several minutes to tug the raft far enough up on the sand to hold. Only then did big Wombo turn to scan the area around the crates already unloaded on the beach.

Carter could read every thought taking place in the man's minuscule brain from the way his flat face contorted, smoothed into puzzlement, and contorted with deep thought again.

Two men . . . were here . . . gone now . . . where the hell are they?

Twin light bulbs went on behind the vacant pupils of his eyes as portable floods bathed the beach and most of the cove in stark white light.

A voice boomed down at them from above, partially muted by a bull horn. "We are agents of the Italian government! You are completely surrounded! Put your hands behind your necks . . ."

That was all he got out. Wombo roared and dug a huge magnum from his belt. The other four men dived for rifles that had been left near the crates but were no longer there.

Carter unslung the Uzi, backpedaled a few steps into the water, and dropped to his belly.

Armed, black-suited men appeared as if by magic from the rocks. They moved forward to the very fringe of the light and dropped into a firing stance.

Behind him, Carter could hear the twin Cummins diesels fire up with a roar. At the same time, he heard the bark of Sophia's Uzi spraying rubber bullets into the rocky cliffs.

The short, staccato bursts from the boat seemed to be a catalyst.

All hell broke loose.

Carter sprayed rubber bullets from his own Uzi high into the cliffs. The men there returned the fire, but high. They wouldn't know which one was Ali Maumed Kashmir, and God help them if they hit him and the whole operation were over before it really got started.

Carter chanced a glance over his shoulder as more black-clad figures emerged from behind the crate and began to charge the Libertà members on the beach.

The powerful Corsair was already flying out of the bay, her bow cutting a high vee through the water, white spume tracking her wake.

Good man, Carter thought, rolling his gaze back to the fray.

Of the five, only Wombo had evidently thought to stick a handgun in his belt. Now he was blindly firing at the figures coming toward him. Most of the slugs were going wild, since the harsh floodlights shone right down into his eyes.

The other four were splitting off, two of them running down the beach, the other two trying to crack the oncoming line of black-clad SID men and gain the darkness and safety of the cliffs.

The latter two were overcome by onrushing bodies. The two going down the beach looked as if they might make it.

Carter sprayed their legs with a burst of the Uzi, and they went down like cordwood. He came up to his feet and sprinted toward Wombo.

The big man's magnum had long ago clicked on empty. Now he was using it like a club, chopping down the SID men as fast as they got to him.

"Wombo!"

"Ugh?"

"This way, follow me!"

"Ugh."

He cracked two more heads and lumbered after Carter. They gained the first plateau of rocks, and Carter spotted a path, the giant right behind him.

They got past the lights and were just climbing toward the last summit, when bodies came down on them from above like huge black raindrops.

Carter went down under a swarm of men. Out of the corner of his eye he saw the beast do the same.

The SID boys were making it look good. They proceeded to beat the hell out of him. Of course they didn't know which one he was, so they weren't discriminating.

Santoni had probably told them: "Work all of them over to make it look good, but don't kill any of them if you can help it. You might kill the wrong one."

Carter played the game until he could feel blood running down his face and knew that his eyes were swelling shut. When the feeling started to leave his back and he was sure he was about to vomit, he gave up and folded into a fetal position on the ground.

The fists and feet gave up on him and turned their attention to Wombo.

Nick Carter could hardly believe his eyes.

There were at least ten men pummeling the big oaf all at the same time. Somehow he managed to mash his way through all of them and take off.

Carter saw his burly outline briefly on the brow of the cliffs, and then he was gone.

Let him go, Carter was thinking. *He'll prop up the story.*

But he couldn't make words through his swollen and cracked lips.

He had just finished emptying his stomach when he was yanked to his feet. A stern-faced, jut-jawed young Italian officer's smiling features were inches from his own.

"You are under arrest."

"Screw you," Carter hissed.

An iron fist in his gut put out the last light.

EIGHT

Italian justice is swift, particularly when it comes down directly from government indictments and the charge is aiding and abetting revolution and arms smuggling.

It was even swifter in the case of Ali Maumed Kashmir aka AXE Killmaster Nick Carter. This, of course, was helped along by the mountain of evidence against him, and the very quiet interventions and urgings of the SID and the even quieter American secret agencies.

His photograph, the face partially swathed in bandages and almost unrecognizable after the severe beating on the beach, was splashed across every newspaper in the world.

His home in New Jersey was raided, and records of ten years of illegal arms smuggling were confiscated. Men in his employ were anxious to testify to save their own skins if Kashmir were brought back to the States to stand trial.

But that would be a long time in the future. Italy wanted him first.

A woman, Naomi Bartinelli, was arrested in New York City and charged with aiding Kashmir in his worldwide arms deals. Several other underground terrorist organizations and business dealings of international crime families were compromised when the woman's computer records were seized in her Manhattan apartment.

Two days after the affair on the beach south of Livorno, Kashmir was arraigned. Three days after that, the trial took place. A week later, he was found guilty and sentenced to fifty years in the maximum security prison, Castel Montferrato.

One piece of strange evidence leaked out during the trial. The SID men had been able to carry out this brilliant raid against the Libertà revolutionaries because of a tip. The leak—that it was an informant—of course was not made through newspapers or to the general public. It was slipped to the underworld and known terrorist cells in Rome, Florence, and Milan.

Clothing, a bag, and papers found in a pension in San Remo clearly stated that the arms had been purchased from a man named Oakhurst in Amsterdam. Oakhurst had tried to cross Kashmir, and he had paid for it with three of his best people.

It was all too apparent to Nicolo Palmori and his lieutenants that this man Oakhurst was the one who tipped the SID.

Two days after the sentencing of Kashmir and the seven members of La Amicizia di Libertà Italiana to Castel Montferrato, a meeting of Libertà leaders was called in Florence.

It was almost midnight when Carlotta Polti parked a Fiat sedan in Florence's Piazza Indipendenza. In the passenger seat beside her sat Sophia Palmori, a blond wig entirely covering her raven black hair.

Wordlessly, the two women got out of the car and crossed the piazza. They reached the Via Zanobi and turned left. The street, lined with well-renovated old houses and an occasional café, was barely two cars wide.

Since it was so late, neither the street nor the cafés were overly crowded. The women turned into the second café they came to.

They sat in a rear booth and ordered wine. When the carafe of harsh local red came, both women poured glasses for themselves but neither drank.

They sat, stone-faced, barely glancing at the well-dressed young people around them.

One by one, three young men came up with open propositions. They were rebuffed or ignored. The men left quickly, and after the third one had made his try, no others approached.

Sophia was the first to rise. She moved through the tables and down the hall to the ladies' room. Inside, she opened the towel holder, withdrew a key from behind the roll, and unlocked a second door marked Storage. She replaced the key and moved into one of the stalls to wait.

Three minutes later Carlotta entered, and both women went through the door, locking it behind them. The stairs were steep and narrow, and they led deep into the subbasement beneath the café and apartments above.

At the bottom of the stairs was another door. Carlotta knocked, and light gleamed through a peephole.

"Yes?"

"It is Carlotta and Sophia."

The door opened at once, and the women entered. It was a large, barnlike room with little furniture. Two iron beds with dirty mattresses graced one corner. A makeshift kitchen with a coffeepot on a hot plate was in another. There was no rug on the bare floor, and the rotting boards looked as if they hadn't been swept in a year.

So went the glamorous life of a guerrilla terrorist constantly on the run.

Above a large round table flanked by several chairs, a bare, low-watt yellow bulb hung, barely illuminating anything outside the sphere of the table.

"My baby!" Nicolo Palmori growled in a whiskey voice, and he folded his fat arms around his daughter.

He planted a sloppy kiss on each of her cheeks and turned to Carlotta, who was forced to undergo the same welcome. Her stomach turned as, over the terrorist leader's shoulder, she saw Wombo take the young girl in his huge arms and invade her mouth with his tongue.

There were two other men in the room besides Palmori and Wombo: Nordo Compari, and a man Carlotta knew only as Pocky.

Both of them were homicidal maniacs and were rarely out of Nicolo Palmori's sight. Compari was almost as big as Wombo, with flat, irregular features, black, greasy hair, and rotten teeth. Pocky had boyish features and unruly blond hair. He was over thirty, but he could easily pass for twenty. His most noticeable feature, other than his vacant blue eyes, was the steel claw he wore in a black leather rig in place of his right hand.

"Sit, sit, everyone sit," Palmori wheezed. "Nordo, pour some wine!"

Carlotta accepted the glass and managed not to wince when Compari's hand caressed hers while handing it over. He had been trying for over a year to seduce her, but Carlotta had always managed to keep him at bay. Once, she had done it by slicing an eight-inch gash across his belly when he was drinking and had tried too hard.

It didn't seem to deter him. He still tried.

Palmori started to rant.

"We must be avenged for this insult! Seven good men in prison because of one pig's petty greed and need for revenge!"

"Eight men," Carlotta said. "Kashmir was almost our sole supplier of arms."

"True, but he too is a pig! Ali Kashmir has served what purpose he had. For all we care now, he can rot in Castel Montferrato with Pietro Amani. But our seven comrades and their revenge? . . . Ah, that is another story!"

As Palmori spoke, his fat belly rising and falling over his belt, Carlotta let her eyes trail around the table. These, she thought, were the remnants of the Libertà leaders. If the necessity hadn't arisen to free Pietro Amani, she would have been able to rig their self-destruction months before.

The only one in the room with any brains, besides herself, was Sophia. And Sophia was obsessed by, of all things, the Libertà cause and sex.

God help the next man Sophia decides to fall in love with after she tires of Wombo, Carlotta mused. The huge beast would probably kill both of them when it happened!

"Do you agree, Carlotta?"

"What . . . ? I'm sorry, my mind was roving . . ."

"Now that we know the identity of this Oakhurst, and where he is, don't you think we should take action?"

"Definitely," Carlotta replied, sipping the bad wine.

Most definitely, she thought. *If one of us takes out Oakhurst, then Interpol, the SID, the Mossad, or any number of other agencies won't have to bother.*

Palmori was outlining a plan. He had nearly finished, when Carlotta realized that she was to be the instrument of ending Émile Dobruck-alias-Oakhurst's useless life.

"But, Nicolo, you have already ordered me to set in motion a plan to liberate our comrades from Castel Montferrato. How can I do that and go to Brussels at the same time?"

"That is true . . ."

Sophia immediately stood, a slanted, leering smile on her lips. "I will go to Brussels," she said, taking a deep breath to expand her large breasts even larger in the too-tight sweater. "It will be easier for me, a *young* woman, to lure this pig anyway."

Nicolo nodded in agreement.

Carlotta thought, *You silly bitch, go!*

"I will go along with Sophia as a backup," Pocky said, lifting his right hand and smiling.

The claw in his leather rig had been replaced by an eight-inch spike.

Castel Montferrato was an awesome fortress perched high above the plains of Alessandria Provence, thirty miles southeast of Turin.

It had been passed down from family to family since the Middle Ages. Now, because of its impenetrable thousand-foot walls, its watch turrets, and its gigantic interior as big as a small city, it was a prison.

No longer did marauding hordes try to breach its four-foot-thick walls from the outside. Now Castel Montferrato kept men *inside* its walls.

Like all Italian prisons, Montferrato was run on the gratuity system. That is to say that if a palm is well greased, the palm will pat the back of the one who does the greasing.

Ali Kashmir was such a one. Because of his notoriety— and his ability to obtain lire from outside the walls—he was exempted from labor and just about had the run of the prison.

Unlike the penal theory of American prisons, where there is ideally some attempt at rehabilitation, Italian prisons are solely for incarceration. But like American prisons, the inmates are thrown into the pool and told to swim as best they can with the other sharks.

Carter learned this only too well the first week. The basic precept of each man was survival. And survival was accomplished only through respect.

The entire center of the compound was a courtyard. Part of the area was for craft shops, where the more skilled prisoners could set up small shops to make and sell their wares to the other, more wealthy prisoners. The rest of the area was used for exercise and recreation, and brawls that decided the pecking order.

It was in the afternoon of his third day that Carter was first tested. He was standing alone, idly watching some of the older inmates playing boccie.

They were goons, two of them. They moved in on each side of him.

"You are the dandy, the rich one, Kashmir, who doesn't have to sweat in the laundry!"

"I am Kashmir," Carter replied in a quiet voice.

"You are not Italian!"

"I am Lebanese."

"Ah, then you sponge off our Italian state! It is only right that you should pay for your food and lodging in this wonderful hotel our government has provided for you!"

"Yes, that's true, Kashmir. We—my friend and I—will collect for the state, each week."

The boccie game had slowed to listlessness, the players now more interested in the drama on the sidelines. A circle of inmates had formed around Carter and the two men challenging him.

Carter looked to the one at his left, then swiveled his gaze to the other man on his right.

"Both of you can go to hell."

One swung a roundhouse right, while the other grabbed Carter's arms and pinned them to his back. He caught the one swinging in the kneecap before the blow landed. The man was still cursing and screaming in pain when Carter kicked again. This time Carter's booted toe caught him full in the face.

His nose spouted blood, and a few teeth dribbled from his mouth as he went down.

The other one, holding Carter, roared and tried to break his shoulders by crossing his arms behind him.

Carter leaned forward, his legs off the ground. He curled his feet behind the other man's ankles and lurched backward.

They both went down with Carter on top, his tailbone crunching into the other man's crotch. His scream of pain made the previous one sound like a whimper, and Carter's arms were free.

He rolled away and to his feet as the first one came up off the ground in a lunge, his face a bloody mask.

The man had about forty pounds on Carter, so the hit was effective.

They both went down, but on the way Carter managed to grab the man's thumbs. By the time they hit, he had curled them both back. Both thumbs snapped like twigs.

This addled the man long enough for Carter to roll him over. Then he sat on his chest and methodically battered his face until it was a pulpy mass.

When there was no movement beneath him, Carter stood and walked back to the second man, who was still rolling on the ground, his hands cupping his ruptured testicles.

Carter was vaguely aware that the other inmates had crowded around them in a tight circle to shield the battle from the prison guards.

Not that the guards would interfere anyway; it made for a better show.

Carter drop-kicked the man in the chest. He rolled over and got two more vicious kicks in the kidneys.

Carter was just sighting in on the back of his neck, when he felt a hand tentatively touch his shoulder.

"Signore . . ."

Carter turned his head. A weathered old face covered with beard stubble was beside him. *"Sì?"*

"I think, *signore*, that if you kick him one more time he will die."

Carter looked at the body at his feet. "Yes, that would be awkward," he murmured.

He stepped away and walked through the silent crowd. They parted like a wave before him and slowly dispersed.

No one paid any attention to the two mangled men on the ground.

That evening, after the six o'clock meal had been served in the huge dining hall, Carter was heading back toward his cell. He was almost there when a ferret-faced little man with droopy eyes and sloping shoulders fell into step behind him.

"Signore Kashmir?"

"Yes?"

"One of the men in the courtyard today . . . Anzio . . . ?"

"What about him?"

"He is in the infirmary. They say he bleeds bad inside. They say he will die."

"So?"

The little man shrugged and smiled, showing crooked and broken teeth. "It matters no more to me than to you if the pig dies, but he has friends."

"And that means that I need friends, right?"

The smile grew wider and uglier. "That is right. In here, there are only two kinds of men, *signore* . . . common pig criminals like Anzio and political prisoners such as myself."

"Headed by Pietro Amani."

"True. Since you already have some affiliation with the Libertà, it would be wise for you to seek out Signore Amani and request his protection."

"For a price, no doubt."

Again the shrug. "Signore Amani respects the fact that you were aiding the Libertà when you were arrested, but in here you must earn your own way. A man like you, with your talent, could be very useful to our side."

"No, thanks."

"Signore Kashmir, Signore Amani does not take no for an answer. He is a boss, and bosses must control."

"Not me."

The grin faded. "This is the only offer that will be made."

"Tell Signore Amani to stick his offer up his ass."

It was about midnight when Carter heard a key being inserted in his cell door. Through one slitted eye he saw Amani's emissary, little Ferret Face, sliding the door to the side.

He was expecting it. *If they won't join you, do away with them.* It was the rule. It maintained discipline. No one is supposed to buck the bosses.

The little man moved like a cat on soft-soled shoes through the door. Carter saw his hand move to his belt, then down to his side.

It would either be a makeshift stiletto or an ice pick. Probably the latter; they were easier to come by. As for the key to his cell, any inmate could get it, with the right bribe to the right guard.

It was the quickest way to solve a problem: an ice pick in the ear and a quiet burial outside the walls.

Carter waited until he saw the arm start down before he reached up with his left hand and locked his fingers around the man's wrist. At the same time, he kicked out and scissored his legs around the man's middle.

When his feet were locked behind the other's back, Carter pulled him in. Carter twisted the wrist around and filled his right hand with the man's greasy hair.

It was an ice pick, and now its sharp needle point was just drawing blood under the man's upthrust, stretched chin.

"Amani sent you."

Silence.

"You're going to die anyway."

"No . . . no . . ."

"Yes."

Carter rammed his shoulder against his left hand, sending the ice pick through the man's throat and up into his brain.

After shutting and locking the cell door, he stuffed the body under the cot. Then he lay down and set the alarm in his head at four hours.

A few seconds after four A.M., he awoke. Ten minutes later the guard passed by, making his last round before dawn.

Carter waited until his footsteps had completely faded before rolling from the cot. He unlocked the door, then hoisted the corpse in a fireman's lift to his shoulder.

On stocking feet, he padded to the end of the corridor and down to the second level. At this time of the morning, sleep was deepest. Not a single head came up from a pillow nor was one snore interrupted as Carter passed the cells with his grisly burden.

Amani's cell was number fourteen on the second level. As silent as death, Carter slid the man's arms through the bars of Amani's cell and secured them with the corpse's own belt.

Five minutes later he was back in his own cell, sound asleep with the door locked and the key hidden in one leg of the cot.

Near the end of the exercise period that afternoon, Pietro Amani groaned into a bench beside Carter.

He was a big man, well over six feet, with a once powerful

athletic body that was now going to fat. Carter knew him to be just past his sixtieth birthday, but he looked ten years younger.

"You are a very relentless man, Kashmir." He spoke without turning his head toward Carter, and his lips barely moved.

"Am I?"

"Removing Guido's body without a report to the warden cost me a great deal."

"Did it now?" Carter dropped the cigarette from his lips and ground it under his boot.

"I don't wish to have a private war with you, and I don't want to see you on the other side."

"You won't."

"Good, I didn't think so. Power is everything in here, don't you agree?"

"I do."

"You and I, we have many years yet behind these walls. You would do me a great favor if you would help me save face by at least nominally giving me your allegiance. I will ask no more of you, and I promise that in the years to come I can help you."

"I don't think so."

Amani's neck began to redden, and his body grew tense. Carter hastened to explain.

"You can do very little for me, Signore Amani, in the years to come, because I won't be here."

"What?"

"I plan on escaping."

The big Italian laughed, a low, rumbling laugh from deep in his gut. "Many have tried, Kashmir, many. And none have succeeded. With bribes we can do practically anything we want in here, but even with bribes we cannot get out."

"I can, and without bribes."

Slowly the mane of gray hair moved until Carter was staring directly into the man's clear blue eyes.

"I think you mean it, Kashmir."

"I do," Carter replied. "If you're a gambling man, you can make book on it."

"When?"

"Within the week."

Carter practically saw the little light bulbs go on behind the man's eyes.

Within a week.

If he could escape, he could usurp Nicolo Palmori's authority and take over the Libertà again. He could meet with the Russians and begin again his reign of terror that would topple the Italian state.

"Tonight, please, come to my cell after lights out."

"Why?"

"Because, Signore Kashmir, if you can get me out of this pigsty and to a certain part of the world in nine days' time, I can put you in touch with certain people who, in your line of work, can make you a very rich man."

NINE

The apartment was in a building that was exactly like its neighbors in the hills above Montmartre. It contained a living room, two small bedrooms, a tiny kitchen, bathroom, and an entrance hall. The furniture was modern and cheap but comfortable.

It was perfect in every way, including privacy and security. Carlotta Polti had checked it out herself in every detail.

It would provide the perfect safe house after the break for herself, Carter, and Pietro Amani, until the old man dictated the next move.

The buzzer rang from five flights below, and Carlotta pressed the button. "Yes?"

"My name is Justin."

"Come up."

She buzzed the voice in and lifted her skirt. Attached to her right inner thigh with a soft chamois harness was a six-inch tube that looked like no more than a chrome pipe with a small plunger on one end. Actually, it was a single-shot pistol that carried a .44 dumdum slug.

From five feet or less, it could tear a man's side out.

Carlotta checked the load, dropped her skirt, and moved to answer the rap on the door.

She gazed through the peephole and then muttered in a low voice, ''Move aside, please.''

''I am alone.''

''I said, move aside.''

He did. When she was satisfied that he was indeed alone, she opened the door and moved back into the living room.

Jason Henry was a king-size man with a florid face that sported a habitual grin and a gleam in the eye that could only be described as mischievous.

''Well, well,'' he said, moving to within a foot of Carlotta and letting his eyes enjoy what they saw.

''You look surprised, Mr. Henry.''

''I am. The scum that usually hires me this way are generally short, fat, beady-eyed, and can barely speak French or English through their slobbery lips.''

''Sorry to disappoint you.''

''Believe me, I am not disappointed. Got anything around here to drink?''

''Wine?'' Carlotta asked, already knowing the answer.

''Wine? Hell, lady, that's for washing down a steak or saying beads!''

''There's a bottle of American whiskey, there, and glasses. Pour me one, too.''

He smiled and rolled toward the table with something akin to a sailor's gait. As he poured the whiskey, Carlotta lit a cigarette and went over what she saw, and what she knew about Jason Henry.

His clothes were far from Parisian chic: khaki pants and shirt with the sleeves rolled to the midpoint of bulging biceps. His shoes were canvas half boots, and he wore no socks. He was a good six and a half feet tall and would never see two hundred and fifty pounds again no matter what diet he used.

Under his roaring manner Carlotta sensed the guile and wit of a true intelligence, and a sensitivity beyond the personality he showed the world. He could have been a New York cop, a New Jersey longshoreman, a Boston politician, or an IRA radical in Cork—anything but an American expatriate on the European continent.

He had served twelve years with the U.S. Army and attained the rank of major in Vietnam. When that war ended, Henry had gone to work for the CIA.

Because of bureaucracy—and the agency not using his many talents—Jason Henry had gotten bored. He resigned, but because of the many contacts he had made, he was able to get work as a mercenary.

Between those jobs, he filled in his time—and his bank account—with a flying service. He was known to have some scruples, but most of them could be stretched with the right amount of money.

Before he had been chosen and contacted by Carlotta, he had been thoroughly checked out on his latest escapades by the Americans and her own SID. Much of what he had been up to had been shady or downright illegal, but that only made him more ideal for the assignment.

Henry handed her a glass and raised his own in a salute. "To the devil and beautiful women!"

Carlotta smiled and raised her glass. "To them being one and the same, Mr. Henry."

"A lady after my own heart!" He drank and smacked his lips. "If we're going to do some hell-raising and head-busting together, why don't you start calling me Jason?"

"Fair enough. My name is Carlotta."

"Carlotta what?"

"Carlotta none-of-your-business. Now why don't we sit down and talk?"

His grin, if possible, widened, and the twinkle in his eyes

got brighter. ''Carlotta, I think I'm gonna like you.''

He took a chair, she the opposite sofa, with a coffee table between them. She spread papers and maps out on the table, and looked up. ''There will be certain preparations to make before the actual mission starts.''

''And the mission?''

''It's in two parts. The first will be to help two men escape from Castel Montferrato, in Italy.''

Henry whistled. ''Sounds like fun.''

''Now, suppose we get down to it.''

She spoke rapidly in quick, staccato sentences, but it still took her over an hour to explain the entire operation with all its ramifications.

When she was finished, Henry got up and poured himself another glass of whiskey. When he returned to his chair, he brought the bottle with him.

''Well?''

''Lady, uh, Carlotta . . . you know what you're asking for?''

''I do. I've just spelled most of it out.''

''You want three untraceable cars to use for carry, lead, and chase. You want three other low-life gunnies that can be trusted, you want to refit a helicopter, and you want the use of my own plane to fly to hell-knows-where.''

''That's exactly what I want.''

''Like I say, you want a bundle!''

Carlotta placed a pad before him, lifted a pen, and wrote a figure. ''I'm paying a bundle, plus expenses.''

Henry looked at the figure and roared with a laugh that practically rocked the room's walls. ''Carlotta, I'm your man.''

She flipped a picture across the table. ''Can you fly this?''

''An H-34? Hell, yes. I flew those banana boats before I knew how to fly props.''

She turned a map around. "This machine is currently here, in a barn about thirty kilometers from the Italian frontier. It needs to be repainted and resignatured. There is also a hoisting device that has been removed but must be reinstalled with a pickup hook."

He nodded. "Probably the same kind we used in Nam. I know it. When does all this have to be ready?"

"In forty-eight hours."

"Jesus."

"Can it be done?"

Jason Henry glanced again at the pad containing the figures and grinned. "It can be done."

Émile Dobruck stepped from the car and crossed the narrow walk to the Club Paris. Without a verbal order, the driver stayed in the car while the two other passengers, Dobruck's new bodyguards, entered the club with him.

At the door, he was greeted with much bowing and scraping, and was escorted to the best table in the house. This was always the case when he was in Brussels and decided on a night out at the Club Paris.

Émile Dobruck owned the club and most of the real estate surrounding it.

His manager, Montchard, saw his boss enter and, knowing Dobruck's taste, immediately signaled the new girl that he had just hired two days before to wait on him.

"Sophie, that is Monsieur Dobruck."

"Yes."

"See that he gets anything he wants . . . anything."

"Yes."

Dobruck caught sight of her before she was halfway across the room headed for his table, and smiled.

Her generous hips moved like a metronome. Above the waist she wore nothing but a thin—a very thin—silk blouse.

It was unbuttoned very low and knotted beneath her ample breasts. She wore no bra, so there was a great deal of creamy flesh exposed almost to the nipples. The nipples themselves, while not exposed, were still visible, twin pink points of firmness pressed against the tight thinness of the blouse.

Below the waist, she wore a pair of hip pants, cut very low in front and back. They were of black elastic mesh.

"I am here to serve you, Monsieur Dobruck."

Her voice was like silk, and the animal heat from her near naked body seemed to flow outward and scorch him.

"You're new."

"I started just yesterday."

"You're not from Brussels."

"No, I am Spanish," she lied.

"And your name?"

"Sophie."

He nodded. "The bartender knows what I drink."

Dobruck watched her move away. She was young and she was beautiful, and because he was who he was, she would be available.

When she returned with his drink, she brushed the mesh covering her hip against his shoulder, again searing his flesh through his jacket.

He fumbled with his wallet.

"There is no charge, Monsieur Dobruck."

"I know," he replied, folding a large note and slipping it into her cleavage. "Perhaps later you will join me for the show."

"I don't know . . ."

"I'll arrange it."

She returned just as the house lights dimmed. In the interim, she had removed the revealing costume and replaced it with a tight sweater and skirt. The street clothes somehow made her look even sexier, and much younger.

Montchard knew exactly what Émile Dobruck liked.

By the end of the show, the girl, Sophie, had made him putty in her hands.

"My house is only ten minutes away," he croaked hoarsely.

"My hotel is only two minutes . . . a short walk."

"But we can be more comfortable . . ."

"No, I'll feel safer in my own room," she replied.

Dobruck was about to get angry. He was about to let her know who he was and what power he had, when he felt her hands on his thighs beneath the table.

Five minutes later they were walking arm in arm from the club.

"This way," she said, turning right. "Who are they?"

Dobruck shrugged. "They are my associates."

"Do they follow you everywhere?"

"Almost everywhere."

"Not into the bedroom, I trust," she said coyly.

"No, my little angel, not into the bedroom."

But almost. One of the bodyguards stayed in the hotel lobby. The other followed them up to her floor and found a chair in the hall.

"Will he just sit there?" Sophie asked, opening the door.

"Unless I need him," Dobruck replied with a leer.

"Let's hope you don't," she laughed, shrugging her jacket off and exiting to the bath. On her way by, she snapped on a radio. "There is brandy on the dresser."

Dobruck poured two glasses of the amber liquid into a glass with quivering fingers.

My night, he thought, already imagining the next hour with this young beauty. *This will be my night!*

And then she was back, dressed in a filmy gown that left nothing to the imagination. She took one of the glasses and moved into his arms.

"You are very beautiful, my dear . . . a young, sensual animal."

"I have Latin blood," she crooned into his ear.

She was light in his arms, and her hair was soft against his cheek. He held her close as he maneuvered her to the bed, and she didn't resist.

She smells of lemons, he thought as the back of her knees hit the bed.

Beneath the filmy sheerness of her gown, he could feel her breasts moving against his chest. Her hips met his, and he shivered at the liquid movement of her body.

"I want you," he growled.

"Are you very rich, Monsieur Dobruck?"

"Very. Rich enough to give you anything you want."

She bent the upper half of her body back in the circle of his arms. As she drained the glass and dropped it to the carpet, she gyrated her pelvis and hips against him.

"Then undress me . . . here," she said, pointing to the sash at her waist.

He drained his own glass, dropped it, and reached with the same hand for the sash. He tugged it, and gasped.

Suddenly the filmy gown was in a heap at her feet, and what was beneath it was a study in olive and pink tones.

A black, lacy bra only just contained the determined thrust of her high-riding breasts, and a black garter belt inadequately straddled the rounded curve of her hips.

She wore no panties, and long, tapering legs supported the breathtaking torso above. Completing the erotic fantasy, and driving everything else from Dobruck's mind, were the sheer black hose attached to the garter belt.

"You are a vision."

"Now," she said, dropping to her back on the bed and spreading her thighs, "undress yourself . . . and take me."

His fingers flew. His eyes were misty, devouring only her

body, so that he didn't see the wide smile that stretched her lips when he dropped the Walther and holster from his shoulder out of reach on the floor.

When he too was naked, he leaned one knee on the bed and began crawling upward over the luxurious softness of her willing body. So filled were his senses with the sight, the smell, and the touch of her, that he failed to hear the bathroom door open behind him.

He was about to enter her, when he saw her eyes open wide. They were suddenly glazed over, and the smile on her lips was like a sneer of defiance.

"Do not be afraid, my dear."

"I'm not," she murmured. "Believe me, I am not."

Émile Dobruck felt only a tiny pain at the base of his neck before Pocky drove the spike inward, severing his spine.

There was no sound, and hardly a drop of blood. Using only the embedded spike for leverage, Pocky lifted the lifeless body off Sophia and let it slither to the floor.

"Hurry!" he said, cleaning the spike on the bedspread. "Dress! We will use the roof. The car is waiting in an alley a block from here!"

Sophia didn't answer. When he looked up, her eyes still held that glazed quality and her body was quivering.

"Sophia, get dressed!"

"No, not yet."

"What?"

She turned to him. "Pocky, take your clothes off."

She lay back on the bed, assuming the pose that she had just assumed in front of Dobruck.

And then he understood.

"Sophia, are you mad . . . ?"

"Yes. Undress, Pocky . . . hurry. We have time . . . hurry!"

It was insane, and yet it somehow fit. Her eyes drew him

like a magnet as he fumbled with his clothes.

And then it was her body drawing him, engulfing him, swallowing him. . . .

Carter moved his hand through the bars, twisted the key around, and seconds later silently slid the cell door open.

Everything was going like clockwork.

Pietro Amani had swallowed it all. Carter knew the whole story, right down to the very time the meeting would be convened.

The only thing Amani had held back was the place. But Carter knew that if Amani expected to be delivered there, he would soon know that as well.

Carlotta and her SID people had come through like champions. The gear that he needed had been delivered early that morning, secreted under the flooring of a van delivering new prisoners. Carter had already transferred it to an abandoned tool shed in the most unused section of the courtyard.

It was three A.M. sharp when he slid on his belly the few remaining feet to Amani's cell and tapped lightly on the bars.

Instantly the old man's face and gray mane appeared at the bars. "You are ready?"

"Yes. Do your people know what to do?"

"They will perform to the letter," the man replied in a whisper.

Carter was sure they would. If they didn't, and that was the cause of failure, the old terrorist would have them visited by an iceman.

"You've put the dummy in the bed?" Carter asked.

"Yes. I am ready."

"Then let's go!"

Using his own key, Amani opened the cell, slipped out, and relocked it behind him.

Together, the two men walked down the tier.

Getting off the cellblock and into the yard would be the trickiest part of the plan. It would have been easier if someone in the prison, either a guard or one of the administrative staff, could have been let in on the ruse. But both Carter and the SID people had vetoed such a gamble.

Graft, bribery, and corruption were too rife. It would have been impossible to be sure that whoever they let in on the plan wouldn't go right to Amani himself and offer to sell the information that he was being broken out by an agent of the United States government.

They reached the end of the cellblock without rousing anyone, and Carter halted. Mentally he thanked the energy shortage. The entire block between the cells was lit by only two low-watt yellow bulbs.

If one of the prisoners had seen them pass, he wouldn't have been able to distinguish between them and guards making rounds.

Where they now stood, there was complete darkness.

"There's a narrow corridor this way, between the wall and the last cell. Grab my belt and stay close!"

Carter moved into the corridor in a half crouch, the Italian on his heels. He made his way about twenty feet by feel alone and halted when his groping hand touched wood.

"Here."

"What is it?" Amani whispered.

"A book of matches. Light one and shield it with your body."

The scrape of the match was like a shot going off in the deathly stillness. The flickering light revealed a four-foot-high door with an ancient padlock.

"What is this?"

Carter spoke as he went to work on the lock. "A few years ago, the powers that be in the prison system decided this whole damned place was a firetrap."

"Which it is," the Italian said with a chuckle.

"Agreed," Carter said, snapping the lock open. "They had to install a way for the prisoners to get down from the third tier to the first, in case the stairs were blocked."

The light flickered and went out. By the time Amani lit another match, Carter had the door open.

"A fireman's pole!" Amani gasped.

"Yeah," Carter said. "It satisfied the safety people, but of course no one bothered to tell the prisoners it was here."

"But when we get down to the first tier, we will still be in the cellblocks."

"No, we won't, because we're not going down . . . we're going *up*. Take your shoes and socks off and tie them around your neck."

"Why?"

"Because the pole is slick—easy to slide down, hard to climb up. You can get more leverage with bare skin."

They both quickly removed their shoes and socks and tied them around their necks. Then Carter lit the whole book of matches and leaned into the hole, holding the light over his head.

"Think you can make it?" It was about forty feet to the top and the trapdoor leading onto the roof.

Amani nodded. "I'll make it. There is still a lot of muscle in this fat."

"Good enough. If you feel yourself start to slip, grab my leg."

Carter dried his hands, blew out the matches, and gripped the pole. Monkeylike, he got the soles of his feet on it and started up.

He could hear Amani behind him already puffing, and hoped the man could last until he, Carter, could get the trap open and lean back to help him.

"You all right?"

"Yes," came the gasping reply. "How much . . . much . . ."

"Farther?"

"Yes."

"I'm there."

The trap creaked like hell when it was opened, but Carter managed to lower it softly to the roof. He jackknifed out of the hole and instantly whirled to dip one arm back in.

"Grab my hand!"

Amani managed to wrap one hand, and then both of them, around Carter's wrist, even as he started slipping back down the pole.

To the old man's surprise, he felt himself being hoisted upward as if his weight were no more than a mere boy's.

Once on the roof, with breath back in his lungs, he turned to face Carter.

"You are very, very strong, Kashmir."

"I know," Carter said, grinning. "Don't forget it in the days ahead. Come on, this way!"

As they ran across the roof, Carter unwound a nylon line from beneath his shirt. He secured it to a ventilator pipe, looked over the side, and dropped it with a hissing sound toward the ground.

"We are over the old part of the yard, where they dump the trash and where the tool sheds for the gardens are located."

"I know it," Amani replied and smiled. "Very wise. The lights here have been burned out for months."

"*Were* burned out. The bastards replaced them the day before yesterday. I spent the whole afternoon today with a slingshot and rocks, breaking them out again."

"How far down is it?"

"About a hundred feet. Can you make it?"

"Going down, Kashmir, even *that* distance, will be easier than what I just did!"

"Good. Here, take one pair of these gloves. The rope is nylon, and even though it's knotted every foot or so, it will burn the hell out of your hands if you slip. And put your shoes back on."

When they were both ready, Carter slipped over the side and began his descent into the darkness.

TEN

Carlotta Polti took one last look at the apartment before dousing the light. A lot had been accomplished out of these rooms in the past few days. A sudden clutch in her belly made her wish, strangely enough, that she could linger.

But that was impossible. Everything had been set in motion now, and nothing could stop it.

As she closed and locked the door, she hoped that she would be alive to see the place again twelve hours hence.

"A franc for your thoughts," Jason Henry said, smiling up at her from the landing.

Carlotta returned his grin. She had grown to like the big American. He made her laugh. "All my thoughts are of lost innocence."

"I wouldn't know about that," he replied. "I never had any. Come along, they'll have our bird ready by now."

On the street, the bright lights of the cafés streamed out to their left at the foot of Montmartre. The sound of laughter mixed with sad, almost bluesy music reached their ears as they walked to the car. A light snow was beginning to fall.

Carlotta had an impulse to grab the big American's arm and steer him down the hill. It would be nice to sit in one of the cafés, drink some wine, and forget, even for an hour.

But they didn't have an hour. Carlotta couldn't remember the last time she had thrown away an hour.

She shrugged off her maudlin thoughts and threw her bag in the back of a little Fiat sedan.

"I would have thought you'd have chosen something faster . . . a Jaguar or a Mercedes," she commented, sliding into the passenger seat.

"Not for a deal like this," Henry said. "This little bucket of bolts is less conspicuous, and besides, if anyone has spotted us, speed won't do much good."

Carlotta was thrown into the seat with the Gs of his takeoff, and then they were swerving and speeding through the narrow streets toward the outer belt of boulevards that would take them around Paris, past the Bois de Boulogne, to the A10. They would take the major artery south to Orléans.

As they passed the Bois, Henry chuckled. "Met my first wife there . . . on a Sunday afternoon. Laid her that night and we got married the following Wednesday."

Carlotta laughed aloud. "She must have been good."

"Oh, she was good."

"Why didn't it last?"

"The poor woman was foolish enough to want me all to herself. I wasn't capable of staying that way. Never have been, probably never will."

"It sounds like you're a sucker for women."

"Absolutely clay in their hands. Gets me into a pot of trouble every time."

"You wouldn't also be referring to the trouble *this* woman is about to get you in?"

He laughed. "I might."

She flashed him a smile in the dashboard lights. "I'll try to get you a bonus. Turn on the heater, will you? It's getting a little chilly."

He reached down and pushed the temperature lever to let

hot water into the heater coils, then opened the floor vents slightly. Carlotta unfolded her legs and moved forward to the edge of the seat to let the hot air blow on her legs.

"Better?"

"Yes, thanks."

"Enjoy it while you can," he said, his face suddenly grim. "It's going to get a lot colder."

"What in hell is all of this?" Amani asked as Carter threw the gear from the shed and began breaking it down.

"These are helium tanks, this is a balloon, this is a nylon and plastic reel, and these are converted body harnesses. Here, climb into this jacket!"

It was heavy and fur lined. "I take it we're going to get a little chilly."

"We're going to go over the mountains into France. If this reel doesn't work, we'll be going overexposed and get *very* chilly."

Amani shrugged into the jacket and lifted his arms at Carter's command. Very carefully, Carter buckled him into the harness, then checked the attachments to the second harness that he would soon climb into himself.

Then he stretched the balloon flat on the ground and attached the helium tanks to its intake valves.

"Here, take this . . . but don't pull on it."

"What is it?"

"A simple little light cord. When the balloon fills and we go up, you pull the cord . . . but not until I tell you. There are two red beacons attached to a large round eye on the top of the balloon. When the beacons go on, they will allow the copter pilot to get his grappling hook into the eye."

"My God, at first I thought we were just going to float over the wall."

"We could, but they would have us in a half hour. In that

time with the copter, we'll be over the frontier into France and gone.''

"Ingenious," Amani declared, gazing up into the black sky. "I hope it works."

Carter chuckled when he saw the sudden layer of sweat break out on the man's face. "It will."

He crawled into his own half of the ribbed harness, and again checked to make sure that all the zippers and snaps were properly secured.

When he was sure they were, he sat down, pulling Amani with him.

"What happens now?" the old Italian asked.

"We wait."

The H-34 sat like a big banana in the lofty old barn. It had been completely repainted, and all of its guns and mounts had been removed.

A fictitious number, as well as the name of a nonexistent flight courier service, had been stenciled onto its brilliant yellow side.

"What do you think?"

Carlotta shrugged. "I don't know. This is your part of it. I assume it's done right."

"It is, but at least you could say it's pretty."

"It's beautiful. How do we get it out of here?"

"We push it."

"What?"

"It rolls like a baby carriage."

It did. Five minutes later, the big machine was on a camouflaged cement pad in front of the barn and they were inside.

Henry went through a thorough but quick preflight, and the rotor above them started grinding around. When it caught, the roar was deafening but then subsided as he adjusted the fuel mixture.

When he was satisfied, he snapped on a light on the dash and adjusted the beam over Carlotta's lap. From behind the seat, he produced a map board and placed it across her knees.

"We'll hedge-hop at two hundred to two-fifty feet until we reach here. I've marked the routes and the coordinates on the map. Watch these gauges . . . altimeter . . . distance . . . direction . . . and keep me informed. Got it?"

"Yes," she said, adding a swift nod of her head.

"When we get here . . . see?"

"Yes."

"We'll have to go up, way up. These are the Graian Alps. We'll cross the border here, at the Mont Cenis Pass. Now be damned sure you keep me above the heights I've noted by watching the altimeter from there on. If you don't, we're in deep shit."

"What does that mean?"

"It means that we crash into the side of an Alp," he screamed over the roar of the rotors as they lifted off the pad, and the nose of the copter swung toward Italy and Castel Montferrato.

Carter was sweating. He checked his watch, sweated some more, and tuned his ears to the sky.

"I don't hear a thing," Amani said.

"Neither do I," Carter replied. "And your boys are about—"

He never finished the sentence. There was an explosion in the opposite side of the courtyard and, immediately following it, the sound of angry, frightened men.

A small ball of orange fire floated into the sky, trailed by gray smoke, and the whole prison was in chaos.

Huge floodlights came on all over the courtyard, and smaller ones danced off the barred windows of the cellblocks.

"They've started!" Amani whispered.

"Yeah. We've got about five minutes and then we've got to go, copter or not."

Carter opened the main valve of the four helium tubes and watched the skin of the balloon start to rise.

None of the lights reached down into the little nook where they were ensconced, but when the balloon was full enough, it would be seen clearly by at least two of the guard towers.

They could hear men, probably guards, running toward the cellblock where all the shouting was coming from.

Three minutes.

"C'mon, get on your feet!"

Amani stood, and Carter clipped the last two straps that would hold their legs together.

"C'mon, dammit," he hissed, "where are you . . ."

Two minutes.

There was no sound from the sky, and now the balloon was starting to take shape above them.

One minute, and the sounds of shouting prisoners grew more intense.

"They're out of the blocks into the courtyard!" Amani whispered hoarsely. "Someone is bound to come this way!"

"I know. We've got to go."

Carter opened the master vent to full, and the balloon started to enlarge at a breakneck pace.

Seconds later, their feet left the ground.

"Here we go. If you're a praying man, Amani, pray that the wind carries us over the wall instead of the courtyard!"

"Blessed Mary, Mother of . . ."

The wind hit the balloon like a giant hand, tightening their harnesses and shutting off their air as well as further speech.

Then the balloon was above the wall, and they were swinging wildly beneath it. The praying paid off. The balloon soared over the wall and kept rising . . . but not fast enough.

"Watch your legs!" Carter cried. "The wall!"

The impact was bone-jarring, but most of it was taken by the bottoms of their feet.

Then they were over and climbing, soaring over acres of trees and skirting the village of Montferrato.

"Kashmir!" Amani suddenly cried. "Do you hear that?"

"Yeah," Carter replied, "from over there."

When he guessed three hundred feet, he killed the valves and yanked the helium tanks free. They spun away into space, and the balloon steadied, riding the wind.

"There it is!"

"Got it!" Carter cried. "Pull the cord!"

Amani yanked on the cord, and nothing happened.

"Christ . . . again . . . be more gentle!"

He did, and two beams of red light immediately whirled above them. Instantly the two guide lights came on beneath the copter. They were hooked directly to the catching hook hanging beneath the nose of the chopper.

All the pilot had to do was drop the hook between the spiraling red beams atop the balloon.

Yeah, Carter thought, *that's all.*

The big machine banked about two hundred yards from them, idled down, and started its run.

"Brace yourself!" Carter yelled. "It's going to be one hell of a jolt!"

Amani nodded, made the sign of the cross, and closed his eyes.

Carter watched the two little red eyes as if they were moths and the bulge above him was the flame.

Fifty . . . twenty . . . ten feet. . . .

He grabbed his harness, tucked his head, arched his back, and. . . .

Nothing.

The chopper whirled over them and away, the blast from the rotors driving the balloon down about forty feet and spinning them like a top.

"What happened?" Amani gasped, holding his head against the dizziness.

"What do you think happened? He missed!" Carter cried. "Get ready, he's coming around again!"

Suddenly the balloon, the dangling men, and the banking helicopter were bathed in stark white light.

Carter quickly swiveled his head. Searchlights from the Castel Montferrato had picked them up. He could see men in the courtyard with rifles at their shoulders.

"They're firing!"

"Yeah, but we're out of range," Carter sighed. "Hang on!"

This time the hook caught and held. Carter thought that every bone in his body had mashed together into one. Amani's eyeballs rolled back into his head, and his arms flew outward from his body.

For a moment, Carter thought the old man had bought it, but then color started to return to his face, and his lips started moving.

"What . . . what happens now?" he managed.

"She attaches the main drop line on these harnesses to a winch, we free the balloon, and we're hoisted up."

The set of red lights went out. Carter unsnapped the drag lines from the balloon to their harness, and instantly the balloon was swept away and down from the blast of the rotor.

Above them, in the open trapdoor, Carter could see Carlotta's face and wildly flying black hair as she finished the tie-off and started the electric winch.

Amani also saw her and grasped Carter by the shoulder. He pointed upward and his lips moved, but the sound was carried away in the rush of wind as they skimmed over the trees at sixty miles an hour.

Carter shrugged and formed the word "Wait" with his lips.

It took a good ten minutes for the winch to bring them up under the belly of the copter. Then the machine tilted and, without the wind as a drag on their bodies, they shot through the bay.

Carlotta closed the doors and turned at once to help them from their harnesses.

"Are you all right, Signore Amani?" she asked, steadying him against her as the harness fell away.

"I think so," he gasped. "Sore, but that's about all."

Carter squirmed from his own harness and helped Carlotta move the Italian into one of the side-mounted bucket seats against the bulkhead.

"Signore Amani, I am Carlotta—"

"Polti. I know, you are one of Palmori's people," he said icily.

"I have worked with Palmori's people, yes, but I assure you that my allegiance has always been to you as our leader."

Amani swiveled his gaze to Carter, who shrugged. "I know nothing of your internal squabbles. I was working with the Libertà when I was arrested. When I requested help to escape, she offered—on the condition that I bring you out with me."

Amani turned back to the woman. "Is that true?"

"It is true. When we get to Paris, and you are able to contact those still loyal to you in Italy, you will find out that I, too, have been loyal."

Amani seemed to accept this and settled back in his seat. Carter grasped Carlotta by the shoulder and nodded his head toward the cockpit.

"Henry?"

She nodded. Carter made his way forward and slipped into the copilot's chair.

"Jason Henry?"

"The same."

"Ali Kashmir."

The head came around with a jerk. "The gun merchant?"

"The same."

"I'll be damned."

"Why do you say that?"

"Because you're a son of a bitch."

Carter had never seen such anger on a man's face. He tensed, fully expecting the other man to take a swing at him. "You know me?"

"Not personally, you bastard. But I hustled a load out of the Yucatán into South America for you two years ago, and you screwed me out of three thousand bucks."

"I guarantee you'll get it," Carter said.

"Great, I'll take it. But once I get you on the ground and I collect, I'm out of this deal. I hate your lousy guts. If the lady had told me who I was gettin' out of there, I would have let you rot. Who's the other dude?"

"Pietro Amani."

"The Italian Commie?"

Carter had to nod.

"Jesus, now I *know* I'm gettin' out of this deal!"

Carter slipped back into the bowels of the chopper and took Carlotta aside. "We've got trouble."

"How so?"

"Henry made a run for Kashmir a while back. Kashmir

shafted him, and he now hates my guts. He also doesn't like the Libertà.''

''Then the solution is simple, my friends.''

It was Amani. He had scooted across the deck and now crouched at their side.

''What does that mean?'' Carter asked.

Amani shrugged. ''Kill the fool when we land.''

Carter had almost started to like the old Italian. Now, in that brief second, he suddenly remembered who he was, and what he stood for.

Carter stepped from the helicopter before the blades had completely stopped rotating. The others followed close behind, Jason Henry bringing up the rear.

A van and a low, sleek Citroën sat about thirty yards away. Three men lounged against the Citroën's fenders, one of them dressed in blue coveralls, the other two in dark trousers and leather jackets.

Carlotta guided Amani toward the van. Henry made for Carter.

''Those are bad boys, Kashmir, but they do what they're paid to do. They'll get you to Paris. The three of you will ride in the back of the van with the guy in the coveralls. The other two will drive the Citroën. It's your crash car if you need one.''

''Are they the same three that we are to use for the second part of the operation?''

''They are, but from here on out you make your own deal with them. I'm out of it, remember?''

As if to emphasize his words, Henry parted his jacket. The butt of a .44 magnum rested directly under his armpit, its barrel almost nudging his belt. The shoulder rig was a split-seam, for fast action.

Carter glanced from the hardware up to Jason Henry's eyes. He was pretty sure the man was an expert with the magnum.

But even if he had doubts, Carter wouldn't have tried to take him. They needed him too much.

"What if I up the ante?"

"Stick it up your ass."

"Amani thinks I should waste you."

"Does he? Why don't you try it?"

Carter smiled and held his hands up, palms out. "If money won't do it, what will?"

"Not a thing, you bastard. I'll do most anything for money, but not for you, or for that guy in the van."

Carter studied the man's cold blue eyes and regular features. He might be a mercenary, but he was obviously one with scruples.

Just their luck.

"Where do you go from here?"

"Take the chopper back to the barn. It's about an hour from here."

"And then?"

"I park it as per our deal. Half the deal is completed. I've been paid half the price. That's it, *finis*."

"What about the money you say I owe you?"

"Keep it. I'll write it off to character development."

"We need you, Henry."

"Well, I sure as hell don't need you. So long, bastard."

Carter made an instant decision. It was all he could do. The entire deal could go sour without this pilot and his connections.

They had come too far to have that happen now.

"Henry, wait a minute."

"Go to hell."

"Goddamn you, hold up!"

The man stopped. He spun around in the same movement, and faster than Carter could see it, the .44 was loose, its muzzle prodding his belly.

Carter looked down, and then up with a smile. "You're good."

"Good enough to kill you if you push much more."

"What if I told you I'm not Ali Kashmir?" he said in a whisper.

"I'd tell you you were full of crap."

"What if I said I'm an agent of the United States government?"

"In Castel Montferrato? Bull!"

"My name is Nick Carter. I work for an agency out of Washington."

Something in Carter's tone made Henry withdraw the gun from his gut. "CIA?"

"No."

"What then?"

"Got a pencil and a piece of paper?"

"Yeah."

"Gimme."

Henry withdrew a pad and pen from his jacket pocket with his left hand. The right continued to hold the magnum steady.

Carter used his knee to write on.

"Here. As soon as you can find a clean pay phone after you land, call this number. Identify yourself and tell them your half of tonight. They'll tell you the rest."

Henry stuffed the pad in his pocket. "Why don't you just tell me?"

"Because you'll believe them."

"Where's the number?"

"Washington," Carter said. "Call it!"

He walked directly to the van, nodded curtly to the hardnose who held the door, and crawled inside.

When they were moving, Carlotta spoke. "Well?"

Carter shrugged. "A little difference of opinion. It's all right now."

"Good," Amani said. "But if the need had arisen, I could have killed him on the spot."

Carter looked down. Amani was balancing a 9mm Beretta between his two hands.

"How long have you had that?"

"Since the first week of my imprisonment at the Castel," he replied with a smile.

"I see," Carter replied, balling his fists to keep them off the man's throat. "Tell me, Amani, would you have shot him before he shot me . . . or after?"

ELEVEN

The sharp click of a heel on the parquet floor brought Nick Carter instantly awake and to a sitting position on the living room sofa.

Carlotta stood in the kitchen alcove, a bag of groceries in one arm.

"Good morning."

Carter checked his watch. "You mean good noon."

He rubbed his eyes and watched her slip out of a fur-lined jacket and place the groceries on a counter. She poured a cup of coffee, placed it and a basket of croissants on a tray, and moved toward him.

Carlotta, Carter mused, was more beautiful than ever. It was as if the danger and excitement of the previous night had made her blossom.

The two top buttons of her shirt were open, her jeans were tucked into high black boots, and her hair was tied back. With no makeup, she looked like a college student.

"Did you sleep well?"

Carter nodded. "Amani?"

"Still sleeping. I just found this slipped under the door."

Carter took the paper from her hand and opened it.

Made the call. Do believe you're legit. Buzz me!
481-776. Henry

Carter handed her the note. "Dial this while I throw some water on my face."

When he returned from the bath, patting his face dry with a towel, she was extending the phone toward him.

"Henry?"

"Yeah. Let's talk."

"Where? . . . Not here."

"I can understand why," Henry said and chuckled. "The Fiat that Carlotta and I used last night is back in its parking space in the alley beside your building. The key is under the driver's side mat."

"All right."

"Do you know Paris?"

"Like the back of my hand," Carter replied.

"Pick me up in an hour on the Boulevard Berthier, in front of Café Trois Roussettes."

"An hour," Carter said and hung up.

"Is it a go with him?"

"Sounds like it," Carter replied, reaching for his pants.

One of the bedroom doors opened, and Pietro Amani—scrubbed, shaved, and dressed—entered the room. "Ah, coffee?"

Carlotta nodded and moved toward the kitchen.

Carter surveyed the man's clothing. "The fit is perfect."

"Yes," Amani nodded. "I am amazed."

Carlotta returned and handed him a cup. "Several people knew your exact sizes. I just added a few pounds because of the time of inactivity in prison."

Amani chuckled. "A wise move." He turned to Carter. "Do we still have an agreement?"

"We do," Carter replied. "I'll get you anywhere you

want to go—for a price, and the certain introductions you mentioned.''

"Good. I'll need to make some phone calls tonight, and probably send a few cables tomorrow morning.''

"The phone is there.''

"No. I'll need a clean pay phone of my choosing—and complete privacy.''

Carter shook his head. "That means you'll have to go out. That could be dangerous.''

"I'll have to risk it,'' the Italian replied and then grinned. "Until I am sure the both of you can be trusted.''

"So be it,'' Carter said with a shrug, rising and moving across the room. He came back with a small case and opened it. "Carlotta will give you a haircut . . . a very short haircut. There is a black wig in here, and other basics to alter your appearance. I assume you don't mind if Carlotta trails you at a distance, in case there is trouble?''

"Of course not,'' Amani said. "But I think it will be myself—Amani—who will soon be creating the trouble!''

Jason Henry waited, slouched against a window of the café. When he spotted the Fiat, he motioned with his head and twirled an index finger one revolution by his ear.

Carter understood, and continued on. He made the turn at the Porte de Clichy, and swung around the large block of the Cimetière Parisien des Batignolles. When he came down Boulevard Berthier again, Henry awaited him on the curb.

He rolled into the passenger seat before the Fiat had even stopped, and Carter was going again before the door slammed.

"Where are we going?''

"Take the road toward Clichy, and I'll tell you what to do after that.''

They drove into the Clichy suburb, and Henry directed him

into smaller and smaller streets until they were on a narrow country road. Finally they stopped in front of a locked gate in a long stone wall.

Henry got out of the car, took a key from his jacket pocket, and opened the gate.

"Where are we?" Carter asked.

"At the far end of Clichy. The house belongs to a friend. Had lunch?"

"No."

"Good."

Back in the car, they rolled through the gate and along a graveled drive that wound through a park filled with flower beds, lawns, and huge trees.

Eventually they came to an esplanade bordered by a low stone wall. Beyond the wall lay a second immense lawn.

"Your friend must employ a lot of gardeners," Carter commented.

"Several," Henry said and chuckled. "Turn here."

The château was huge, with a red tiled roof, a broad terrace, and a private lake in the rear.

They scrambled from the car, and Carter followed Henry into a marble-floored, tapestry-hung entrance hall.

"Jason, you are back! Luncheon is ready on the terrace!"

Henry's friend was tall and willowy, with a face and figure that could have stepped directly off the cover of *Vogue* or *Elle*.

"Celeste, I'd like you to meet my friend, Monsieur Carter."

"Welcome to Château Rombouard, Monsieur Carter." The woman smiled warmly. "Are you, too, in the export business?"

"Non, mademoiselle," Carter said, returning the smile. "I am merely a salesman of insurance."

"No matter. Any friend of Jason's is always welcome."

She turned to Henry. "Take Monsieur Carter to the terrace, *mon chèr*. I will have luncheon served immediately."

As she wafted away, Carter put it all together. "Countess Celeste Rombouard," he murmured with a low whistle. "You travel in some pretty classy circles!"

Henry shrugged. "It pays, in a foreign country, to have powerful local friends."

"Lovely lady."

"She manages to keep me warm on cold nights. Come along."

Lunch was delightful food and chitchat, but Carter was glad when it was over.

"I'll leave the two of you to brandy and business," the countess said. She pecked Henry on the cheek and disappeared.

He lit a cigar and motioned Carter to follow him. They walked to the middle of the huge rear lawn and sat in a flower-bedecked gazebo.

"I got the whole story, Carter. You got a tiger by the tail."

"Yeah, I think I do," Carter agreed. "But if I can find out where this meeting is, and get something substantial on who's there and why, you can imagine the lever."

"I sure as hell can. Are you sure Amani won't cross you when the time comes?"

"No, but it's a chance I'll have to take."

Henry nodded and sipped some of his brandy before he spoke again. "I've done a little checking on my own. In my business, you know most of the people who crawl through sewers."

"I suppose you do," Carter replied wryly.

"Word's out from Italy that Palmori and his bunch are mad and scared as hell. The Libertà factions split into two armed camps the minute it hit the papers that Amani was sprung."

"We figured on that."

"It won't be long before they'll figure he's in France, and probably Paris. They'll have a contract out on him . . . and probably on you, too."

"And Carlotta," Carter added. "She was supposed to use Palmori's money to get the other Libertà members out, not us."

"How does she fit?"

"Italian SID."

"That figures." Henry paused, his clear eyes boring into Carter's face. "I'll give you three days in Paris before the guns start coming out of the woodwork."

"Hopefully we won't be here that long. That's where you come in."

"Where to?"

"I don't know yet. And I won't until Amani gets it all together. He starts making his phone calls this afternoon."

"My first thought is still to get the hell out of this."

Carter shrugged. "Your choice, but I can sweeten the pot."

"With Uncle Sam's money or Amani's?"

"Amani's."

Henry finished his brandy and took a long pull on his cigar. "Then I'm in. The number I gave you is here at the château. You still have it?"

"Yes."

He stood. "Keep me posted."

"I will."

Celeste Rombouard met them at the front door. "Ah, Monsieur Carter, you must leave us so soon?"

"Yes, I'm afraid I must, Countess," Carter said. "The lunch was excellent."

"*Merci*," she replied with a graceful nod, then placed her hand lightly on his arm. "We are planning a small get-together this weekend—a few passé nobles, some politicians, an American millionaire or two. It will be wonderful laughs. Please come!''

Carter hesitated for a moment, then shook his head. "I'm terribly sorry, Countess, but I fear I will be abroad . . . on business."

She threw up her hands in mock despair. "Ah, business is such a bore! I keep telling Jason to retire, but he says he doesn't want to be a gigolo and live on my money!"

Carter grinned. "Perhaps, Countess, if our business goes well, Monsieur Henry will be able to retire on his own money."

Nick Carter drove leisurely back to Paris. Carlotta was playing Italian mama when he arrived at the apartment, in the kitchen, elbow-deep in pasta.

He heard the shower running in the bath.

"Amani?"

She nodded. "It's the second shower he's taken since we got back. He says it's necessary to get the scum of Montferrato off his skin."

"He's a many-sided old man," Carter mused.

"He's a revolutionary terrorist with an ego that will allow him to do anything," Carlotta said icily. "I see only one side of him. I've seen his victims."

"*Touché*. How went the afternoon?"

"Well, I think. He made four calls, each lasting at least fifteen minutes. From the amount of coins I saw him drop, at least three of them were out of the country."

"What was his mood after the last one?"

"Absolutely jovial. We had a drink and lunch, and he treated me like a long-lost daughter."

"Then he trusts you?"

"Completely, I think. But then he should. I laid the groundwork well."

"Did he mention—?"

"—when we leave?" It was as if she read Carter's thoughts. "Yes, the day after tomorrow."

"But not where?"

"No. But I've warned him that if the distance is great, extra tanks must be installed on the plane. We must know ahead of time."

"Ah, Kashmir, my friend!"

Carter turned. Amani was lumbering through the living room, vigorously rubbing his now much shorter gray hair with a towel.

"Amani," Carter said.

"I want you to get me a number of flight maps. The list is there, on the phone table. Ah, Carlotta, pasta! Tonight we feast!"

Carter read the list: Switzerland, France, Italy, Spain, North Africa.

My God, Carter thought, *it could be anywhere*.

Pietro Amani had wasted no time recementing his control over the Libertà.

The next morning's Paris dailies, as well as the *International Herald Tribune*, carried the story of Nicolo Palmori's assassination. It had taken place in a cellar under a café and apartment house in Florence.

Nordo Compari and two underlings had been killed along with him.

After reading the accounts, Carlotta had a single, terse comment. "That leaves Pocky, Wombo, and Sophia Palmori . . . all of them more dangerous than the old man himself."

"And with revenge added to their bloodlust," Carter said, "they'll be even deadlier."

A half hour later, Amani emerged from the inner sanctum of his bedroom and beamed over the news stories.

"Retribution is sweet" was his only comment.

Carlotta retreated to the kitchen. Carter steeled himself.

"If we're leaving tomorrow night, Amani, I'm going to need some information today."

"You will have it. First, here are the cables I want you to send this morning."

Carter took them, gave them a quick read, and nodded noncommittally.

They were gobbledygook; all resembled letters of no consequence to friends or old family members. They were signed "Father," and their destinations were Bern, Rome, Frankfurt, and Cordoba.

"I'll get them off right away," Carter said. "I hope the one to Switzerland is my money."

"It is," Amani replied. "The account number is encoded within the text of the cable."

Carter was surprised. Amani's fingers still reached a lot farther than the boys in the AXE think tank had surmised.

"What else?"

"Signore Henry's plane is still hangered in Orléans?"

Carter nodded. "A private—*very* private—strip just south of the town."

"Excellent."

The old man smoothed a large piece of onion skin between them.

It was an intricately drawn flight plan from Orléans to X. It had altitudes, distance, approximate flight time, and codes for international clearance.

The only problem was X. There were no identifying landmarks, or names of cities or villages, to give Carter a hint as to the direction in which they'd be flying.

"What about coordinates and landing facilities?" Carter ventured.

The old man's smile was impish, with one eye blinked

shut. "I will give you those when we are safely in the air."

"You're a careful man, Amani," Carter said.

"Very. I was lax and trusting just once in my life. It cost me the years in Montferrato. I won't be so foolish again."

Carter shrugged. "It's your party. I'll need seed money today."

"I called in a letter of withdrawal to my Geneva bank. You can pick the funds up anytime today at Credit Suisse here in Paris."

"Under the DuBain name?"

"Yes."

Eric DuBain was on the new passport Carter had picked up the previous evening, courtesy of the Paris AXE office. He also had acquired passports under new names for Carlotta and Amani.

"That's it then. I'll get to Henry."

"And I'll make my final calls."

Amani retreated to the bedroom, and Carter joined Carlotta in the kitchen.

"Watch him like a hawk. He's a smart old bird, and there's no telling what he might try to pull."

"I will."

"If anyone—I mean *anyone*—gets close enough to pass him something, or even whisper to him, get a picture!"

"You can count on it."

"I'm ready!" Amani called from the living room.

"Good luck," Carter murmured as Carlotta moved through the kitchen door.

They were barely out the door, when Carter was at the phone, dialing.

"Oui?" It was Celeste Rombouard's musical voice.

"Countess, I would like to speak to Jason, please."

"Ah, Monsieur Carter, I recognize your voice. It is like basso at the opera! Jason is sleeping at the moment. Is it important?"

"It is."

"Then I shall awaken him. One moment."

It was about five minutes before Jason Henry's raspy, sleep-filled voice came on the line. "Yeah?"

"How'd you do?" Carter asked.

"Cars and guns are ready. The plane is set. All I need to know about are the tanks and clearances. Also, I should file a flight plan for Customs by tonight. Where the hell are we going?"

"That's still in the dark." Carter sighed heavily. "I need to see you this afternoon. Where can we meet?"

"Call you back in two minutes."

The connection was broken. Carter got a fresh cup of coffee and lit a cigarette. They were both half gone when the phone rang again.

"Yeah?"

"There's an alley called Bedouins Row, off rue Germain in Pigalle. Do you know it?"

"No, but I'll find it."

"At the end of the alley is an erotica shop. Go through the rear curtains and up the stairs. It's a whorehouse. Her name is Madame Zola. Use the DuBain name."

"Got it."

"An hour?"

"Make it an hour and a half. I have to pick up the loot."

Carter hung up and moved into Amani's bedroom. It took him five minutes to find the flight maps, and another five to learn nothing from them.

The rest of the room revealed nothing. If Amani made notes, they were either in his head or on his person.

He dressed quickly and drove the Fiat toward the Champs-Élysées.

The Swiss tellers carefully scrutinized the amount of the draft and his passport, and then gave an audible sigh as they passed it back.

It hurt them to give out money.

"How would you like it, *monsieur* . . . a draft?"

"Cash."

"Cash, *monsieur?*" The man's face was pained.

"Cash, all kinds of bills."

"That will be a large amount . . . bulk, *monsieur* . . ."

"I have a briefcase."

When it was full, Carter asked to be directed to the rear exit of the bank. "I'm sure you understand."

"Oui, monsieur."

Carter exited the bank and walked the few blocks to the Étoile métro station. He took the Number 2 line and got off at Pigalle. Once he located rue Germain, he bypassed it and walked all the way around a six-block stretch, entering from the other end.

Because of his pace—fast, slow, fast, slow, with a lot of window shopping and a pause for an ice—he was positive that, if he had picked up a tail, he had also lost it.

The alley was just that, wide enough for two people to pass, and dark as night in the middle of the day.

A couple of seedy-looking pimp types working dexterously with fingernail clippers gave him a hard once-over as he went into the garish shop.

The clerk, looking like a graduate student at the Sorbonne, looked up, nodded, and went back to his textbook.

Carter perused nude women, nude men, nude men and women, and a few magazine covers for about five minutes, and then headed for the rear curtain.

"Monsieur?"

"Madame Zola."

"Oui, monsieur."

Carter spotted the man's hand hit a button under the counter, then went on through the curtain.

The stairs were lighted by a series of bright red bulbs.

The French, he thought, *are wonderful. They believe in tradition.*

A steel door opened just as his foot hit the top step.

"Monsieur?"

"Madame Zola?"

"Oui."

"I am DuBain."

"Come this way."

She was very wide and easy to follow. They moved down a hallway lined with doors both open and closed. Carter could hear mewling, cooing, and an occasional groan of either passion or desperation from behind the closed doors.

"Monsieur Jason is in the S&M suite, right here." She opened a door and stepped aside. "Go right in!"

Carter did, and the door closed behind him.

There were a lot of chains and leather on the walls, garish red carpet and drapes, and a huge circular bed with a black leather spread.

In the center of the bed was Jason Henry with a bottle of wine and a plate of cheese.

"Well," Carter said, looking around, "this is depressing."

"Glad you like it," Henry said, rolling off the bed and seating himself in one half of what looked like an iron maiden. "Now, what have we got?"

Carter handed over the flight plan. Henry smoothed it out and produced a navigational computer and his own charts of Europe.

Carter took a seat in the other half of the torture device and lit a cigarette.

A half hour later he asked, "Well?"

"Tough."

Carter continued to chain-smoke and helped himself to a few slugs from the wine bottle. Twenty minutes later, Henry got up and paced, rubbing his eyes.

"This is going to take some time. There's a continuous sex show at the end of the hall . . ."

"I'll wait here."

It was another hour before Henry turned the charts and Amani's carefully drawn flight plan around and revealed his findings.

"All right," he said, wetting his throat with a fast swig from the wine bottle. "We've got five ways to go, based on flight time and fuel, along with his altitude designations. I'm assuming Italy's out. Both of you are too hot there."

"Good assumption," Carter said.

"Germany's out; the mountains there don't have the altitude indicated on his flight plan. And England's out, even if he were trying to trick us by asking for more gas than he needs."

"So that leaves . . . ?"

"Over the Swiss and Austrian Alps to here, just short of Vienna . . . or over the Pyrenees to here, southern Spain."

Carter remembered the cable to Cordoba. "Try Cordoba."

Henry did some quick figuring, looked up, and nodded. "It would fit. Also, we're only crossing one frontier . . . much less risky."

Carter mulled over the charts, then shook his head. "If it is Cordoba, I would guess it's a jumping-off place. That many high-flying terrorists coming into Spain would be spotted."

"Then my guess is he's setting himself up some secondary transportation, to here."

Carter watched the point of Henry's pencil fall on the northern tip of Algeria, and nodded. "That would sure as hell fit."

"And if that's the case, Amani has already called ahead for a welcoming party for us in Spain."

"It would seem so." Carter stood and stretched.

"So what do we do?"

"We go," Carter said. "It's all we can do."

He hefted the briefcase to the bed and opened it.

"There's your payroll . . . plus."

"Pretty," Henry sighed. "Very pretty."

"How far can you trust the guns you hired?"

"With the Crown Jewels, as long as they get paid."

"Okay," Carter said. "We leave at ten tomorrow night."

TWELVE

Carlotta and Amani left by the rear door of the apartment house. They were picked up three blocks away by Jason Henry in the van.

Carter went over the roofs and dropped down into a small back street a block away. The big black Citroën was waiting with its motor running.

"What's your name?"

"Maurice."

"Do you know the route?"

"*Oui.*"

They rendezvoused just past the Bois with four more guns in a Renault sedan. Just south of Paris, they turned off the A10 and found the old road to Orléans, Route 20.

"Where will the van be?"

"Just short of Arpajon. There is a rest stop."

Just outside Paris, a misty rain turned to sleet. When Maurice the driver turned off the highway, the sleet was quickly becoming snow.

Carter noted that the Renault had sped on by the cutoff.

There were two cars besides the van in the rest area. When

the car stopped, Carter slid from the passenger seat and entered the building.

Jason Henry was already at a urinal.

"Any trouble?"

"None. You?" Carter asked.

"We're in business. I'll lead you out."

"Good. What about the other two cars out there?"

"Couples . . . kids who can't afford a hotel room," Henry explained with a grin.

Going out, Henry climbed into the driver's seat of the Citroën, and Carter veered to the van.

Amani was on the passenger side, his Beretta in his lap. Carlotta was at the rear doors, cradling an Uzi. In the driver's seat was another Beretta, compliments of Henry. Carter shoved it in his coat pocket and climbed into the van.

No one spoke as Carter pulled in behind the Citroën and they headed south. About three miles on, the Renault pulled in behind them to form the caravan.

Halfway between Arpajon and Etampes, it started snowing heavily.

"Can he fly in this?" Amani asked.

"We have a check stop at Angerville," Carter replied. "We'll make a weather call."

He flipped the wiper switch to high, and they settled back in silence. Carter could hear Carlotta's long nails in the rear of the van tapping the barrel of the Uzi.

There were few cars on the road, and everyone was driving cautiously. Carter himself had slowed down, taking the curves at a slower speed and accelerating less as he pulled out of them. A wall of snow seemed to settle around the van, isolating them in a cocoon of white. Even the alternating forests and open fields on each side of them seemed distant as the car carved a cave through the falling flakes.

"Goddamned idiot!" Carter snapped as another van, dark

blue with blacked-out windows, whirled around them and cut back to the right lane in front of them much too soon.

There was a tense moment as Carter saw the other van charge the taillights of the Renault. For a brief second, he thought that the driver of the van—even though he was closer—didn't see them.

Then the van swerved out and was around the Renault, speeding much too fast down the highway.

They passed through Etampes, and just south of the town, Carlotta crawled forward.

"Ali . . . ?"

For a bare second, Carter didn't respond to his alias. Quickly his eyes darted to Amani to see if the old man had caught it. He was napping.

"Yes?"

"That van was parked in Etampes, outside a bistro."

"I saw it. Did you notice the woman in the passenger seat?"

"Yes, but I couldn't tell if it was Sophia. But she does wear a blond wig."

"We'll compare notes when we stop in Angerville."

When Carter emerged from the restaurant, the snow had receded a little but still fell in a steady pattern. The cold, now damp air was heavy with the reek of gasoline fumes and the smell of coffee from the sack in his hand. Now and then the heavy rumble of a truck reached his ears from the highway.

The Renault had already gassed up and moved to the south end of the drive. The van was still at the pumps, and the Citroën was at the north end of the drive, near a phone booth.

Jason Henry was in the booth.

Carter passed the coffee through the window of the van. "Stay alert. I'll be right back."

Fingering the Beretta in his pocket, Carter walked toward

the parking lot at the edge of the building.

He walked all the way around the restaurant building to the adjoining gas station and stood, out of the snow, in the lighted bay. The second parking lot was also devoid of anything suspicious.

"May I help you, *monsieur?*"

It was a young boy fixing a tire in the bay.

"Non, merci," Carter said, and then changed his mind. He pulled a pencil and the Michelin road map that he and Henry had pored over in the restaurant from his pocket, and approached the boy. "Perhaps you can at that. Do you live in this area?"

"Oui, monsieur."

Ten minutes later, Carter approached Henry just as the other man stepped from the phone booth.

"Well?"

"It had better be Spain," Henry replied. "This mess is moving in a blanket north and northeast. If we get off the ground, the only way to go is south."

"Okay. Get your artillery out of the Citroën, put it under your coat, and join us in the van."

"Something wrong?"

"Just a hunch," Carter replied. "There was a CB antenna on that van that passed us and stopped at Etampes. They haven't passed again, but they could be tracking us. If anything pops on down the road, I think it would be best if we were all together."

As they walked to the van, Carter played a penlight over the map. Besides the published routes, there were now penciled lines crisscrossing back and forth across Route 20 and the nearby A10 superhighway.

"What's up?"

"Who knows?" Carter said and shrugged. "But remember what you said about being spotted if we stayed in Paris too long?''

"Yeah?"

"We might have stayed too long. You drive!"

Henry gunned the engine and steered from the parking lot. He flashed his lights, and once again the Renault took the lead, with Maurice and the Citroën close behind. On the highway, they quickly gained speed and the Renault's tail-lights faded in the snow.

Suddenly a small sports car whirled around them and immediately slowed.

"Bastard!" Henry hissed and hit his horn.

"Can you pass him?" Carter said.

"Not in this crap. We're losing the Renault!"

Carter leaned his eyes to the back windows. He couldn't see the headlights of the Citroën.

"I don't like it," he growled, jacking a shell into the chamber of the Beretta. The sound was answered by a similar click as Carlotta readied the Uzi.

"There's something ahead!" Henry shouted. "Christ, it's a roadblock!"

Carter scrambled forward.

There were no cars in sight, but two stanchions had been raised on their lane of the road, with red lights atop them and a gate between. Three uniformed men were beside the road, but through the snow it was impossible to tell what uniforms they wore.

The sports car was already stopped at the gate. There was no sign of the Renault.

"Amani, get in the back!"

"Do you think it is the police, looking for us?"

"Move!" Carter barked. He could hardly tell the man that he knew damned well it wasn't the police.

Just as Carter slid into the front, Henry stood on the brakes.

"Look, there in the trees!"

Carter looked. It was the ass end of the Renault sedan. At that second, the sports car took off and then skidded sideways in front of them. Two of the three uniformed men drew their guns and started running toward the van.

Carter took one of them out right through his side window, and Henry wrestled the steering wheel. By the time the van was all the way around, Carlotta had the rear doors open and the Uzi was barking.

"In the little sports car . . . ?" It was Amani at Carter's shoulder.

"Yeah?"

"Sophia Palmori!"

"Let's hope the Uzi nails her," Carter said, already running his penlight over the map. "There's a side road up here about two miles. Take a left!"

The words were barely out of his mouth when twin headlights hurtled out of the snow directly toward them.

"It's the blue van!" Carter shouted.

"Dammit, they must have gotten Maurice!" Henry cried, managing to swerve just in time to avoid the other vehicle.

He took the corner in a skid and saw a clear ribbon of unmarked white leading to the A10.

"Jesus, I hope there's a road under that," Henry muttered, then dropped the van into high gear as he floored the accelerator.

There was, and it was solid under the white powder.

"What now?"

Carter consulted the map. "There's an underpass. Just on the other side of it, take a left. It's an on-ramp to the A10."

Carter hung on to the seat and the door handle until he was satisfied with Henry's driving ability and they were skittering half sideways up the on-ramp. He then screwed his body

around in the seat and looked between Amani and Carlotta.
He saw light at the bottom of the on-ramp, and then the hazy
yellow of the other van's two fog lights.

"What's that?" Henry asked.

"Them," Carter replied. "They're coming after us."

They hit the A10 south at sixty miles an hour, and Henry
did everything he could to urge more speed out of the vehicle.
Beside him in the passenger seat, Carter was again consulting
the map.

"They must have a supercharger in that thing," Henry
said. "They're gaining by the second!"

"I know," Carter said, looking up at a passing sign and
quickly back down at the map.

"Wonderful. So now we're in up to our ass!"

"Watch the road and drive, Henry."

Again, Carter peered through the back windows. The
distance between the two vehicles was growing shorter by the
second.

"He's good," Henry said. "A little too good. We'll never
outrun him."

"I told you I know that," Carter replied.

He slid from the passenger seat and made his way to the
rear of the van. He took the Uzi from Carlotta's hands,
ejected the magazine, and jacked in a new one.

"Carlotta, you and Amani swing open the doors and hold
them open when I tell you! Henry . . ."

"Yeah?"

"There's a sharp curve just ahead. When you get beyond
it, slow down!"

"Gotcha!" Henry replied with a resounding laugh, already seeing Carter's intent.

They started into the turn and, halfway around, caught a
patch of ice. Luckily Henry was already gearing down, so it
was easy for him to right the van and make the turn.

"Now!" Carter cried just as he saw the fog light beams come around. Amani and Carlotta threw the rear doors open and held them with their legs.

At the same spot in the turn, the other van caught the sheet of ice. But its speed didn't allow for the same reaction Henry had been able to make.

Carter narrowed his eyes against the gusts of cold air and swirling snow that filled the back of the van, and started spraying with the Uzi. He caught the left front headlight, and saw the slugs stitch a path across the fender, the door, and then shatter all the windows of the van.

There was a screaming cry of metal as the van hit the guard rail and careened by them on the shoulder.

By this time, Henry was crawling. When he came to a complete halt, Carter rolled from the back of the van, with Amani directly behind him and Henry pouring out the driver's side.

Just as Carter had hoped, the sudden reversal to an offensive position had left the other van's occupants stunned. He was ten feet from the rear of the van and running, when the doors suddenly opened. A monster crouched behind them, the magnum in his two hands looking like a toy. He got off one slug before Carter sprayed with the Beretta.

He was looking right into the big man's eyes just before they disintegrated.

The passenger side door of the van opened, and two men tumbled out as Carter fired another burst. To his left, he heard feet pounding on the snow-covered pavement. It was Henry, already firing his own Beretta. He nailed the driver right through the side window and hit the front fender as Carter cleared the back of the van.

Less than half a minute had elapsed since the initial crash.

There was a bank beyond the guard rail, with a drainage ditch at the bottom of it. Carter jammed a fresh magazine into the Uzi, took the guard rail in a dive, and rolled.

He drew no fire by the time he hit the ditch, so he chanced a look over its edge into the woods beyond.

Still no fire.

He rolled over the embankment and crawled into the trees for about twenty yards. The thick fall of snow had been hindered by the heavy foliage of the trees above. Those same trees now blocked out any light from the van's headlights above.

Carter took two steps forward, and a boyish-looking man with a claw for a right hand rolled around a tree ten yards in front of him.

The claw was across the trigger of a machine pistol.

Carter stitched him across the chest just as a blur of movement drew his eyes to the right.

It was Amani, and the barrel of his Beretta was pumping saffron flame. He emptied the whole clip into the second man who had been crouching in a praying position twenty yards behind Carter's victim.

The man groaned once and folded. When Amani reached him, he kicked him in the side as though he were still alive.

"Bastard," he hissed, then reloaded the Beretta.

"Wombo is in the van, dead. That was Pocky you just killed."

It was Carlotta at Carter's elbow. "And the other three?"

"They look like French, probably locals that Sophia hired in Paris."

"And Sophia?"

Carlotta shook her head. "I tried at the roadblock, but I think I missed her."

Carter shrugged and moved back up the bank. "Henry!"

"Yeah?"

"Will their van move?"

"I think so."

"Knock out the other headlight and drive it over the embankment, through the hole they already knocked in the guard rail."

"Gotcha!"

Carter moved back toward their own vehicle, Carlotta and Amani close at his heels. He slid into the driver's seat as they climbed into the back.

The sound of grinding metal had barely subsided before Henry was settling into the passenger seat.

"Let's go!"

They moved, and five minutes later found themselves hurtling south on the A10 toward Orléans as fast as the van could carry them.

Past the city, Henry gave Carter directions to the airfield. It was little more than a dirt strip cut into a small farm field. The hangar was an open barn.

Carter rocked the van to a halt and turned to Amani. "Okay, now we have to know where the hell we're going, because we might not be able to go. Tell him, Jason."

"This storm is going north and east. If you're thinking about Switzerland, Austria, or Germany, forget it."

Amani smiled. "We'll be going south, gentlemen . . . to Spain."

"Where in Spain?" Carter asked impatiently.

"Near Cordoba," the Italian replied, then leaned forward, placing the Beretta just behind Carter's left ear. "I assure you, Signore Kashmir, I have trusted you up until now . . . but—just in case—I want you and Henry to pass your guns to Carlotta."

Carter barely managed to suppress a smile as he passed the Uzi and the Beretta over to Carlotta Polti.

The last words she had whispered to him before she and Amani had slipped from the Paris apartment were rattling around in his head: *He's not going to kill you or Jason, but he's going to have you held while the two of us go on.*

And when you go on, Carter thought, *I'm going to be right behind you!*

At Amani's orders, Carlotta buried all the guns except the Beretta he held. Henry checked out the plane while Carter transferred the bags.

"Believe me, Ali Kashmir, I am not double-crossing you. I am just unable to take you all the way with me. You and Henry will be completely paid when we reach Cordoba."

"And the other half of our agreement? The introductions to certain people?"

"Ah, I fear that was a little white lie. You see, one day soon, those *certain* people I spoke of will not need to buy their arms from you."

The plane was a twin-engine Beechcraft. It would carry six easily.

Henry was already in the cockpit and had the propellers turning when the rest of them climbed inside.

"I am sorry we must soon part on a sour note, Ali," Carlotta said loudly enough for Amani to hear.

Carter shrugged. "As long as I get paid. And I've always enjoyed Spain . . . particularly on a paid vacation." He leaned forward and patted his canvas flight bag. "I even brought my camera along!"

Carlotta smiled. It was she who had slipped the camera into the flight bag early that afternoon, after an AXE agent had draped it over her shoulder in a métro crowd with Amani not twenty paces in front of her.

Carter glanced forward. He could see that Jason Henry was seething.

Quickly, he stood and moved around Amani into the right seat. While he was buckling in, he flipped the radio toggle to "headset" and whispered, "Cool it!"

Henry's eyes widened and then narrowed. "That bitch," he whispered. "She screwed us!"

"No, my friend. The game is being played quite nicely."

THIRTEEN

The strip was little different from the one they had taken off from in France: a wide patch of cleared ground in a farmer's field.

Just before landing, Amani had given instructions to Henry: "Radio Cordoba that you are having engine trouble!"

Henry radioed the message twice, along with the coordinates that Amani gave him. Then the old Italian had leaned forward and ruptured the radio jacks with a screwdriver.

"Now you may land. The coordinates are miles from here, near the Portuguese frontier. That's where they will look for you!"

Henry landed the plane with only a couple of hops on the rutted, hard-packed dirt, and taxied to the end of the makeshift runway.

There was no hangar, just a couple of olive sheds, and between them stood a strutless Cessna 210 with an Arab-looking pilot lounging against the fuselage.

"Our new chauffeur is waiting, Carlotta," Amani chuckled.

Four men with machine pistols surrounded the plane as Henry rolled to a stop and cut the engines. Three of them were Spanish or Arab, dressed similarly in black leather jackets and dark trousers. The fourth was in a baggy dark suit and looked to be Scandinavian or Slavic.

It was Slavic.

Carter detected the Russian accent in the man's English when he embraced Amani and they exchanged greetings.

The Russian gave the same greeting to Carlotta when Amani introduced them. Then, one by one, Amani shook hands with the three leather-jacketed gunmen.

It didn't take a genius to figure out that they were Basques from the north, probably members of the ETA's renegade terrorist arm.

Amani went into a subdued, heads-down conference with all four of them. After a lot of head-shaking and a few smiles, the Italian walked back toward Carter and Henry.

"Signore Kashmir, you have proved invaluable. But as I told you, I cannot let you accompany me on the last leg of my journey."

"So they waste us," Carter growled, nodding his head toward the four men.

"Quite the contrary," Amani replied, chuckling. "They will merely hold you here until I have landed at my destination. It should not be more than four hours at the most."

"And then?" Henry asked between clenched teeth.

"Then you will be released to continue your flight to Cordoba. What both of you do then is your own business. Your money, Signore Kashmir, has already been transferred in Switzerland. You see, I am a man of my word."

"One of those men is Russian, Amani," Carter said. "Is that who you're dealing with now?"

Amani frowned, but only for a second. Then his lips spread in a wide grin. "I have made my peace with my Russian comrades. With their help, I will have Italy. It is what I have always wanted."

The three leather jackets stepped forward and motioned

Carter and Henry toward one of the olive sheds with their guns.

Carter grabbed his flight bag, and the Russian started squawking, *"Nyet, nyet!"*

Carter looked quizzically at Amani. "I'm as wanted as you are. I'll need my disguises and a change of clothes to go through Spanish Customs in Cordoba."

Amani nodded and calmed the Russian's fears. "The lady and myself removed all their arms before we left France. The bags have also been searched."

The KGB man nodded reluctantly, and they were hustled to one of the olive sheds.

When they were inside and the door was locked behind them, Henry whirled on Carter.

"What the hell is going on?"

"No more than I expected," Carter replied. "Did you get a good look at that Russian's eyes while Amani was talking to us?"

"You bet your ass I did."

"And what did you see?"

"He's going to waste us the minute Amani and the woman are gone!"

Carter nodded, watching the activity outside through a crack in the boards that had been nailed over the single window. "My sentiments exactly. And I'll go you one guess further. I'll bet they plan on burying us up here in the mountains somewhere and using your Beechcraft themselves."

There were olive crates scattered around the shed on the hard-packed earth floor. Henry flopped down on one of them and sighed.

"You know, Carter, this is really not the way I figured to go."

"You're not going anywhere but out of here." Carter sat

on another crate and began digging in his flight bag. "Get up to the window and tell me how they're moving outside. My guess is they'll come for us as soon as the Cessna is off the ground."

Henry moved toward the window, but he seemed not to hear all of Carter's words. "And that little bitch, Carlotta . . . I thought you said she was Italian SID!"

"She is," Carter replied, lifting a heavy camera case and tripod from the bag. "And she's a damned fine actress."

"She's a bitch! They're warming up the Cessna."

"We had to play it this way because we didn't know the final place of the meeting . . . exactly *where* Amani was going."

"We still don't."

"We will. And when we do, I've already set up a way to contact Carlotta. You see, Henry, Amani now trusts her. With her on the inside, I can get the exact information I need."

"Which is . . . ?"

"Breaking up this little get-together is important, yes. But more important is getting the facts and proof that the KGB plans on aiding and abetting. If we have that, we can tie all their hands!"

Henry turned back from the window to face Carter. A light bulb seemed to flash on behind his eyes.

"And you think Carlotta can get close enough to get that proof?"

Carter smiled. "She's very experienced and very beautiful. Yes, I think she can. And when we find out what the proof is—and *where* it is—you and I will figure out how to get it."

Henry suddenly realized that Carter was pulling an expensive Rolleiflex camera apart and deftly reassembling the pieces in his lap.

"What the hell are you doing?"

"It's a specially altered 9mm parabellum model 951 Italian Beretta. Its operation has been redesigned from delayed blowback, semiautomatic, to full automatic. The barrel length has been shortened to three inches but beefed up to handle drilled, semimagnum loads. Its muzzle velocity is still better than a thousand feet per second, and the four-load magazines can be chain-locked, end to end, up to five, so they will spring-feed twenty shells. These sections of the tripod are actually loaded magazines."

Carter linked the magazines together, snapped the top one into the butt, and sharply pulled the slide to jack a live shell into the chamber. Then he held it up so Henry could see the final result.

"And *voilà!* It becomes a minisubmachine gun weighing less than a pound and a half!"

"I'll be damned."

Outside, the Cessna's engine roared and the plane began taxiing. From the alternating sounds, both men could tell when the little plane had lifted off.

"Okay, the goons will be coming soon," Carter hissed. "Stand directly in front of me when they come in. Roll when you feel the barrel of this baby in your back!"

Carter explained the rest in short, biting sentences, with Henry nodding his understanding.

A key in the padlock outside the door brought them quickly together.

"Ready?"

"Ready," Henry whispered.

The door opened. Two of them came in single file and then spread out, one covering with his machine pistol, the other advancing to get behind them.

Carter waited until the advancing man was just in front of Henry, then he grazed Henry's back with the Beretta's short barrel.

Henry dropped like a felled tree and rolled as the Beretta

began to chatter. Neither of the men had time to blink before they met their Maker.

Six 9mm slugs caught the first one in the chest. As he reeled back and down, Carter kept firing. One slug took his chin away on the way down, and five more slugs went over his falling body to make a corpse of the second one.

He had barely hit the dirt before Henry had his machine pistol, then Henry and Carter were out the door and running.

The third leather jacket was pumping fuel into the Beechcraft. Henry went at him full tilt as the man made a dive for his gun ten feet away on the ground.

He never made it.

Henry cut him in half vertically, from crotch to sternum, just as his fingers found the gun.

"Where's the other one? The Russian?"

"You got me," Henry shouted in reply, dropping to his belly, foot to foot, with Carter.

Both of them played their guns in an arc in their halves of the circle.

They were about to stand, when an engine roared to life and a small Seat sedan flew toward them from behind the second olive shed.

"Turn him before he gets the plane!" Carter yelled, coming to one knee.

Both guns chattered. Slugs ripped across the front of the fenders and the radiator. Steam immediately engulfed the front of the car. But now they had the range.

The windshield shattered, held for a second, and then flew completely apart. Behind it, the KGB man lay back in the seat, his arms wide, half his face gone.

But the car came on.

"Get the tires!" Carter shouted.

Both guns sprayed the front end again until the car slumped

and started to swerve. It teetered on two wheels, then rolled completely over to its side, to the roof, and back to rock on its wheels.

"Finish gassing the plane," Carter growled. "I'll clean up this mess!"

He dragged the two bodies from the shed and stuffed them into the Seat, then joined them with Henry's kill.

By the time he had finished, the Beechcraft was fueled and Henry was rolling the portable tank out of the way.

"Don't shut it off," Carter said, taking the hose from his hand. "Get aboard!"

Henry nodded and headed for the plane. Carter dragged the portable tank to the Seat and drenched the car. He then made a twenty-yard trail of gasoline away from the vehicle and pushed the portable tank back close enough to the Seat so they would both go off together.

He made a makeshift fuse out of a gas-soaked handkerchief and a book of matches, and raced for the plane.

"Jesus, you're thorough," Henry said, jamming the throttles forward.

"Less explaining to do. Think we can catch them?"

"No problem. We're pretty sure they'll head south over the Med, right?"

"Right," Carter agreed.

"Okay, I can triple their speed, and probably more than that on altitude. They're probably flying low to go in under radar. Fix one of those jacks and get on the radio to Cordoba tower."

"New flight plan?"

"Right," Henry said, banking the plane into the wind. "We'll file for Marrakesh. That's far enough south in Morocco that we can probably go anywhere legally, while they have to play games."

They were just lifting off when the Seat exploded behind them.

"There he is!"

Carter leaned forward. It took him several seconds to spot the gun glinting off the Cessna's silver skin.

"He's banking."

"I got him," Henry said, throttling back and trimming after setting his rpm.

They watched the smaller plane roll toward the foothills of the Atlas Mountains where they met the sea. Suddenly the banking stopped, and the Cessna was literally hedge-hopping the low-level mountains.

"Well, we know one thing," Henry declared. "It's Morocco. That is, if that crazy bastard doesn't fly into the side of a mountain!"

Both men held their breath as the Cessna pilot rolled over the edge of a plateau, let his air speed build going into a valley, and then trimmed again as he barely made the next peak.

"What do you think?"

Henry shrugged. "It's all desert. He could land anywhere, once he gets over these mountains."

"But it's going to be near Fez or Marrakesh, right?"

"Has to be. That's all there is between the ocean and the mountains."

Henry climbed a little more to make sure they weren't spotted, and they both settled back in their seats to play cat and mouse.

The old capital of Fez dropped away far below and to their right. Then it was endless sand for another half hour until, on the distant horizon, they spotted the red city of Marrakesh.

"They're landing!"

Carter craned his neck, pasting his eyes to binoculars.

The Cessna set down on a ribbon of red clay road that wound down from the foothills of the Atlas and on into the desert. With the prop still turning, Amani and Carlotta alighted from the plane.

"Can they see or hear us?" Carter asked.

Henry shook his head. "We're too far away for them to hear over the Cessna engine, and we're right in the sun."

Carter nodded, and watched a car scoot forward from a small Berber village about eight miles from where the Cessna had come down.

By the time the plane was taking off again, the car had reached the couple.

"Follow the plane for a little," Carter commanded.

Henry did, until they were both sure of its direction and probable destination.

"Algeria?" Carter asked.

"Looks that way. The guy can really fly, and he obviously knows these mountains. He's probably been running a taxi service around here for years. Why Morocco for this big confab?"

"My guess is easy access from Algeria, Libya, and the sea. Also, it's neutral ground and a melting pot for tourists. Any nationality can blend without standing out. Let's get back to the car!"

From a long distance, they followed the dust trail of the little sedan until they were sure of its destination.

"I'd say Marrakesh," Henry said.

"I'd say you're right. Double back to Fez and land there, just in case. We'll drive down. You have any Moroccan connections?"

Henry laughed. "Friend, I've got connections everywhere."

"I figured," Carter said. "Get me on the ground. I've got to find a telephone!"

FOURTEEN

The peaks of the High Atlas Mountains were snow-covered in the far distance. It was dusk, and as the sun dropped farther below the horizon, the sky turned a glowing orange. Flights of egrets and other birds swooped low over the red roofs of the city, coming home to roost for the night.

Carter, wearing dark glasses and a set of small-power binoculars, sat on the roof of the Café des Mille et Une Nuits. He sipped a glass of mint tea and watched the five o'clock rush of tourists and natives in the square below him.

He rested his arms on the parapet and looked down onto the multicolored human carpet that covered the huge open marketplace of the Djemma El Fna.

The square was packed. Besides the vendors' open stalls, there were the fortune-tellers, the fire-eaters, the snake charmers, and the storytellers, each surrounded by a rapt audience.

And in the center of it all was the backdrop and the stage of the Conjuror.

Carter adjusted the glasses to a snake charmer and his helper working just at the edge of the Conjuror's stage. The helper looked like a light-skinned Berber from the mountains. His robes were multicolored: saffron, blue, and gold.

They covered his entire body and half of his face, and above the cloth that draped the bridge of his nose, Carter could see the alert eyes darting everywhere—much as Carter's were —examining each passerby.

The snake charmer's helper was Jason Henry.

The man had proved to be more than up to any task Carter put before him.

It was the fourth day since they had arrived and set up shop in three rooms of a cheap hotel on the Avenue Mohammed V.

Local CIA and AXE people had been brought in from Casablanca to do the legwork. But when it came time for the tricks to start, it was Henry who knew how to recruit.

Carter hadn't been surprised to find that Amani had taken rooms in the poshest resort hotel in Marrakesh, the Mamounia. The man might be struggling for socialism, but he hadn't completely given up his taste for capitalist comfort.

KGB locals were everywhere, but it had been a simple matter to slip the means of contact to Carlotta on a breakfast tray the second day.

That afternoon, she had avidly watched the snake charmer after leaving the door of the tailor shop on the far side of the square.

Every evening, over a hundred pickpockets moved through the square, preying on the tourists. Two of them now worked for Henry.

After a nod from Henry identifying Carlotta, the youths went to work.

Carlotta never felt so much as a tug on the purse slung over her shoulder.

Ten minutes later, several dirhams passed from Carter's hand to the youths, and the Killmaster was reading her note:

There are over forty of us, and three KGB representatives. We are staying all over the city, some outside the city. We will be given a new route each day, but the meetings are always in the same place. Beneath the shops on the west end of the square is a huge cellar warehouse. It belongs to a rug merchant. It is there.

Every word is carefully recorded, and if any settlement is eventually reached, I think it, too, will be recorded and signed. I think these documents are taken to the same place each night and locked away. I hope to find out soon where.

Wherever it was, Carter guessed there would be a safe and a vault. That night after dinner, he gave Henry a complete list of materials he might need.

The man was a genius.

By midnight, everything was safely gathered and hidden away in their rooms.

The next day, the communication process was repeated. This time, notes were exchanged. Carter had written out, in exact detail, what Carlotta was to do when the time came.

The boy took only minutes to make the trade and return to Carter's side.

"Merci."

"Very pretty lady. Yours?"

"Not really."

"Too bad. You want woman tonight?"

"Not tonight."

"Too bad."

The boy shrugged and left, and Carter unfolded the note.

Nothing new on the place of safekeeping, but I'm getting closer. I can't wait to be with you again.

• • •

Carter paused, felt a tug at his groin in memory of when they were last together, and then continued to read.

Amani and I have discussed our plans of departure when the time comes. I think it will work out well.

The next afternoon, the purse was empty. Carter sighed. Now it was a waiting game.

He removed the glasses from his eyes and rubbed the burn from them.

The thin wail of reed pipes, the beat of drums, and the sounds of cymbals in the popping fingers of belly dancers wafted up to his ears.

There was sound and movement everywhere. Acetylene flares were already being lit on many of the stalls in anticipation of the coming darkness.

And then he saw her.

She was moving through the crowded square like a tall, raven-haired goddess in a lightweight white cotton dress. She paused only a moment in front of the snake charmer's mat and reached into her purse.

Carter held his breath.

Then a bright red and gold scarf settled over her hair, and Carter sighed with relief.

It was the signal.

The meetings were over and the agreements had been signed. She had the information.

It was all over, and it was time to go.

Instead of nodding to the youthful pickpocket, Henry swiveled his head and threw a glance at the turbaned Conjuror, who was already going into his act next door.

Carlotta moved on to stand in the first row in front of the stage, and Carter screwed the glasses tighter to his eyes.

The Conjuror started his spiel. His eyes in the gaunt,

bearded face under the gaily colored turban seemed to rake the crowd. Then, after an interminable time, they fell on Carlotta.

He was off the stage in an instant and tugging her forward. She pulled back, shaking her head and looking around at the crowd in embarrassment.

Carter could see the magician's lips moving rapidly, urging her to join in the fun. He gestured to the crowd for them to add encouragement.

They did, with exuberant chatter and applause.

Carlotta capitulated.

The magician guided her to a large, upright box at the rear of the stage and placed her, standing, inside. Nervously, she looked out at the crowd as the man began his mumbo jumbo.

He walked around the box, twirled it for the crowd, and then banged it to show that it was solid.

Then the door was closed and locked. A huge black curtain was draped over the box, and the Conjuror was again going through his gestures and incantations.

Carter shifted his glasses.

Henry and the snake charmer had already packed up. Carrying a huge straw basket between them, they were quickly making their way through the crowd.

He moved the glasses to the other side of the stage. A donkey cart of canvas-covered straw was already moving through the stalls.

The Conjuror gave the box one last final spin, and two assistants lifted the black curtain. The donkey cart was just passing behind the stage as the box was being unlocked.

Carter was already going down to street level when the door opened and a dark-skinned, scantily clad dancer stepped from the box, her belly rippling and the cymbals on her fingers jangling.

•   •   •

Carter cracked the door of the room when he heard the grunting on the stairs. When Henry's head appeared above the landing, he yanked it all the way open and darted into the hall.

"Any trouble with the switch?"

"Not a bit. Give us a hand!"

Carter helped them into the room with the basket. The snake charmer disappeared back down the hall, just on the outside chance that they had been spotted.

Henry closed and locked the door as Carter lifted the lid on the basket.

"Oh, God," Carlotta moaned. "I could hear the snakes in there crawling around under the false bottom! Have you got a drink?"

"I sure have," Carter said, giving her a quick kiss on the lips and pouring her a whiskey.

She downed it in one swallow and held out the glass for another.

"What have you got for me?" he asked as he refilled the glass.

She stepped from the basket and moved to the bed, where she dumped the contents of her purse. From the mess, she selected a lipstick tube and pulled it apart. From one end of it came a tiny roll of paper.

"Here is a list of everybody there . . . their names, aliases, and the approximate times of their departures tomorrow. I was only able to get about half of the methods and routes."

Carter took the paper and hugged her. "It will do." He passed the paper to Henry. "You know what to do with that?"

"I sure as hell do."

Carter turned back to Carlotta. "Now, my dark-haired Italian beauty, what else have you got for me?"

"It's a jeweler's shop dealing in very expensive, high-class gems. Here's the address."

Carter memorized the address, burned the paper, and turned to Jason Henry.

"You know what to do from here on, Jason. Take good care of her. Now it's my own ball game."

"Nick, does this mean . . . ?"

She had grasped him by the shoulders and spun him around.

"It means, Carlotta, that I won't see you until sometime late tomorrow afternoon. But you can do something special for me."

"What?"

He leaned forward until his lips were right at her ear. "Be bathed, perfumed . . . and naked."

With a chuckle, he grabbed a dun-colored djellaba and a pair of sandals from the bed, and was out the door before she could reply.

It was around ten o'clock when Carter reached the new part of town. He had shuffled all the way from the small hotel in the Medina and moved through the crowded souks to make sure he had not been followed.

Beneath the dun-colored djellaba that covered him from the top of his dark head to the sandals was the package of material that Henry had procured days before.

The shop Carter sought was on an old street in the new part of the city. It was one that was going through the transition from cheap and run-down to quaint and prosperous.

The street held a few teenage boys on the prowl and a few prostitutes trying to get the boys interested. The traffic was disturbed by a sudden light rain that had just begun to fall from a heavily overcast sky.

Carter moved to within two doors of the shop, and had

stepped back into the shadow of a doorway to light a cigarette, when he spotted a patrol car approaching. He pulled the hood of his djellaba up against the rain and slid to a sitting position as the car came abreast.

The eyes of the two policemen combed the street from side to side through the rain-streaked windows. A spotlight flicked on, and Carter tightened himself into a ball and lowered his chin into the robe.

The spotlight swept by, paused, then returned. Carter felt a cold, hard knot forming in his stomach as the glaring light bathed him, shining through his closed eyelids. His breath came in quick gasps. It was common knowledge that the police would stop and sometimes search loiterers in the area for drugs.

With what Carter had concealed under his clothes, there was no way he could stand a search. If the car stopped and they got out, he had already decided that he would have to make a run for it and come back later.

The car's engine muttered throatily as it idled, then the spotlight winked off and the car moved forward again. The cops were evidently reluctant to get out in the rain for what appeared to be a beggar sleeping in a doorway.

Carter uncurled from his crouch and crossed the street to another doorway opposite the building housing the shop. Through the rain he spotted the tiny, darkened mouth of an alley on the far side of the shop. He waited for two cars and a pedestrian to pass, then he moved across the street and into the alley.

All of the first-floor windows were protected by heavy steel bars, and the windows adjacent to the fire escape on the rear of the building had shutters of heavy wire mesh that were locked on the inside.

He climbed up the fire escape to the roof, then scaled over the parapet and walked slowly across the roof, peering around in the dim light. There was a shedlike structure in the middle of the roof, with a door in one side. It was evidently the access to the stairway leading downward, but the door was of heavy metal construction and locked from the inside.

Kneeling in front of the door, Carter opened his djellaba and then his shirt. From around his middle, beneath the shirt, he unwrapped a wormlike rope of magnesium plastic. Dividing it into two equal lengths, he wrapped the protruding door hinges with the plastic and sheltered a match in his hands to light it. It sputtered, caught, then began burning with a glaring white light, illuminating the building with a blinding, flickering glow.

Carter shielded his eyes from the light, looking worriedly around at the adjoining buildings in case someone could spot the intense illumination. No lights showed at any windows, and suddenly the magnesium flickered out.

The door sagged toward him as he edged his fingers into the crack at the top and tugged. He gently slipped it out of the frame and braced himself against the heavy weight. When it was safely lying on the roof, he went down the steps. At the bottom, there was a landing and another door. He froze in his tracks when he saw light coming from around the cracks in the door.

Was the light coming from around the door just a night light?

Carter knelt and put his ear to the door, listening intently. Moments passed, and the only sound was the drumming of his own heart. He turned the knob and pushed. The door opened, and he rolled into the room, doing a 360° turn before coming back to his feet.

The room was empty. A small lamp burned brightly beside a cluttered desk.

Quickly, Carter produced a canvas bag and went through the office. Other than simple personal articles of some value and some cash, very little else went into the bag.

The second floor was more productive. He went through the showcases, taking only the articles of value that would interest a professional thief. Everything on the second floor was factory-made, such as standard rings, necklaces, brooches, and watches.

The first floor was another showroom of locked cases, and a comfortable lounge where clients could enjoy a drink or a buffet while selecting their purchases or ordering a specific item.

Through curtains in the rear he found another, smaller room that appeared to be no more than storage space.

Carter guessed there was more.

Behind a ceiling-high set of crates, he found a trapdoor. From here on he would be flying blind. It only stood to reason that the real goodies were somewhere in the basement. Everything of value in Marrakesh was stored somewhere below street level.

The basement seemed to consist of only a storage room. Then, in the light of his flashlight, Carter noticed a thick bundle of wires in the corner of the stairwell ceiling. Carefully, he traced them. They disappeared through the wall in a corner behind a pile of Bedouin antiques, adjacent to a strong, heavy door not unlike the one he had blown on the roof.

Another rope of magnesium plastic was pressed into service, and two minutes later he was in the goodie vault.

Raw gold, gems, and two trays of antique coins and assorted jewelry went into the bag. Then he pulled a stethoscope from under the djellaba and went to work on the real object of his search: an eighteen-inch Bennington minivault built into the four-by-four concrete section of the wall.

Carter had guessed as much. If the vault-within-a-vault hadn't been a Bennington, he was sure it would be a one-unit, self-contained safe of similar indestructible construction.

It was only the German firm of Bennington that did a large security business in Morocco.

To crack this one would take more magnesium and other chemical explosives than Carter could have carried. And then there would be a good chance that the room would be in shambles, the concrete would be rubble, and the hingeless, seamless tank of the small vault itself would be lying on the floor, completely intact.

Besides, Carter thought as he went to work with the stethoscope and his talented fingers, his aim wasn't to burglarize the safe for the purpose of theft.

It took nearly four hours before he heard the twelfth and final tumbler roll into place with a barely perceptible click. By the time he tugged the door open, his fingers were numb, his senses were raw, and his whole body was bathed in sweat.

Only one sweep across the shiny steel interior and he found what he was looking for amid velvet cases of priceless gems.

The box was made of steel, with a double combination lock. Compared to the safe lock he had just conquered, these two were child's play.

He lifted the lid with bated breath, then sighed in relief.

They were all there, carefully filed and indexed by a master sheet. He didn't know a few of the Russian designations, but most he did.

Carefully, he rigged a light with a special high-intensity bulb above one of the gem trays, and then he began to spread the documents.

He photographed a set at a time and very carefully replaced them in the folder.

The photography took another hour, but the time was worth it.

When he was through, he made sure that he had left no trace that he had been inside the vault proper. When this was done, he relocked the door, reset the timer, and returned to the first floor.

At the rear of the building there was a heavy steel door that gave access to and from the alley. He felt above the door with his fingers until he found the wire connecting the trip to the burglar alarm. With two wire-connected alligator clips, he bypassed the breaker and then attached one end of a large spool of twine to the wire.

Satisfied, he unlocked the bolts and chains that secured the door. He gently eased open the door, and sighed at the silence.

He had found and shorted the right wire.

The alley was still and quiet, with only the sound of the rain pattering down and the gurgle of water in the gutters and drainspouts.

When his bag of loot was safely rolled and secured to his belt under the djellaba, he stepped through the door into the alley.

Carefully, he moved toward the street, playing out the twine behind him. The area in front of the building was deserted, and the rain was falling harder now. Carter went on across the street, then yanked at the twine.

The alarm filled the rain-sodden night air instantly.

He quickly rolled the twine as he walked. By the time he reached the corner, it was a neat ball in his hand. He shoved it into his pocket and turned onto a more heavily traveled street, glowing yellow with the light from cafés.

He spotted the dark, official-looking car—a Renault with diplomatic plates—a block in front of him.

He shuffled toward it and darted into the passenger seat before the young driver was even alert to his presence.

"Ashburn?"

"Yes, sir."

"I'm Carter. Let's go!"

The car roared to life, and they were speeding toward the northwest sector of the city.

"How long a drive to Casablanca?"

"About two hours. I might be able to make it in an hour and a half this time of night."

"Make it in an hour and a half. Does your radio work?"

"Yes, sir."

"Phone ahead," Carter said, crawling into the backseat, "and have somebody get someone in a photo lab ready to go."

"I take it then, sir, that we've got them?"

"Son, we've got them by the balls. Wake me on the outskirts of Casablanca!"

"Yes, sir!" the young man whooped. "May I be the first, sir, to congratulate you?"

Carter didn't hear a word the young foreign officer said.

He was already sound asleep.

FIFTEEN

At precisely noon, Ronald W. Hatfield, vice chairman of the American legation in Casablanca, Morocco, sat down in a well-padded chair in an outer office of the legation of the U.S.S.R. in Casablanca.

He waited fifteen minutes before a stocky blond woman in a skirt and blouse that somehow looked like a uniform emerged from behind two tall teakwood doors.

"Chairman Hatfield?"

"Yes."

"Comrade Chairman Zalenkov will see you now."

"Thank you."

Hatfield moved easily through the doors and was warmly greeted by Igor Zalenkov.

"Ronald, it's been two weeks since tennis. How about Saturday?"

"Marvelous, Iggy. Lunch first?"

"I am sure I can make it. The Foreign Club?"

"That would be fine, Iggy."

The two men had known each other for three years. They often played tennis together and, with their wives, dined in the finer restaurants of Casablanca and Rabat.

"Well, Ronald, what can I do for you?"

"I'm afraid this one is distressing, Comrade Chairman."

"Ahh, real business," the Russian said, accepting the sheaf of papers being passed across the desk.

He perused them for five minutes, and when he looked up again, clouds covered his face.

"I assume there are several copies?"

"There are," Hatfield said. "A full set should be in Washington within the hour. We could, if necessary, have them at the U.N. by morning, New York time."

"I see. Will you excuse me?"

"Of course."

Ronald W. Hatfield smoked a small cigar while he waited. It didn't burn far down before Zalenkov was back in the office.

"I presume you have demands?"

Hatfield handed him a typed list.

"I have to say these are impossible," the Russian replied after a quick perusal.

"Of course you do. But, Igor, I do suggest that you get back on your code machine while I'm here."

Zalenkov nodded and exited the office again.

Hatfield was just extinguishing the cigar when he returned.

"Yes?"

"Agreement."

"Complete?"

"In every detail."

Hatfield snapped his briefcase shut, shook hands, and moved to the door.

"Ah, Chairman Hatfield . . . ?"

"Yes, Chairman Zalenkov?"

"I probably won't make tennis on Saturday."

Hatfield nodded. "That's to be expected, Iggy. Perhaps another time."

''Yes, perhaps . . . let's hope so.''

Zalenkov had scribbled on a pad. He passed it to Hatfield.

DAMN THE KGB

Hatfield wielded his own pen.

I QUITE AGREE

Thirty-three men and women of foreign nationalities, all with forged passports, were detained at various border stations.

One of these was Petro Amani, just as he was about to board an Air Maroc flight to Vienna.

He didn't resist, but walked silently between the two uniformed officers. They exited the terminal and entered the parking lot. They were halfway to a police van when a young, attractive blond woman disengaged herself from a clump of people and moved in behind them.

When she was two steps from the prisoner, she pulled a Mouser from beneath the trench coat she wore and held it in front of her face.

''Amani the Pig!'' she screamed.

Amani and both officers whirled at the same time.

''Sophia . . .''

The Mouser held a twelve-round clip. She managed to put eight of the large-caliber slugs into Amani's body before she died herself from the officers' returning fire.

Jason Henry deftly guided the powerful little launch through the breakwater.

Six miles south of Casablanca, he docked at a private pier. Two long tiers of wooden steps led up the side of a hill to a charming villa.

Henry jumped ashore and held the launch as Carter stepped to the pier.

"My God, it's beautiful."

"You've got it for a full two weeks."

"Where do I send the rent check?"

"You don't," Henry said, back in the launch, already revving the engine. "It's called Villa Rombouard!"

Before Carter could reply, Henry was gone, heading out into the bay.

She was waiting in the center of a large living-dining area. Behind her, a table was set with fine china and candles.

"Welcome home."

"For two weeks, I'm told," Carter replied, moving toward her.

"I've already prepared dinner . . . for later. We will begin with *saumon fumé* and proceed to *truite à la hussarde* and *délices de sole d'Antin*. From there it will be a romp through *ris de veau* and *étuve de boeuf maconnaise*, all complete with various side dishes, and served with vintage wines of the Rhine, of Burgundy, and finally, champagne."

"It sounds delicious," Carter said. "And in the meantime?"

He was directly before her, his lips almost touching hers.

"In the meantime, I am bathed, and perfumed, and"—Carlotta shrugged her shoulders, and the wispy robe slithered down her body—"and naked."

DON'T MISS THE NEXT NEW
NICK CARTER SPY THRILLER

THE BLUE ICE AFFAIR

The hallway was lit, though dimly. It was in the shape of an L, the staircase running up from its center.

Carter walked silently down the corridor leading to his room. The possibility of danger had yet to dawn on Aubrey as she followed behind him in silence. It must have registered when he reached for his holster and drew out his 9mm Luger, affectionately called Wilhelmina.

"What . . . ?" Aubrey began.

He turned and placed the tip of his index finger to her lips. *I don't know*, his eyes answered. *I just don't know for certain*.

The door to his room was closed. The lights were out as he had left them. He checked the lock to see if it had been tampered with; it hadn't been touched. But waves of intuition warned him that something was wrong.

Carter stood to the side of the door, then put his ear to the wood. Inside, he could hear the whispered command of one man to another. He was right. Perhaps it had been Van der Grif's warning that Andrei knew of his presence in South Africa, or the information he'd received with regard to Aubrey's true identity, but something had alerted him. His hunch was on target. The tentacles of the Soviet KGB had extended into South Africa. Indeed, they had extended into his very room and were waiting there to put an end to his life.

"Stay here," he whispered to Aubrey. "And whatever happens, don't make a sound."

She nodded woodenly. Her face was white.

Carter trotted to the end of the hallway where a casement window faced Schaumberg Avenue. A narrow ledge ran around the hotel, punctuated by balconies that protruded from each of the streetside rooms. Covered with stucco and enclosed with fancy wrought-iron railings, they had been long neglected and seemed incapable of supporting much more than a few potted plants. Still, if he used the ledge as a catwalk leading to the balcony outside his room, there was an excellent chance he'd be able to catch his would-be assassins unawares.

Carter opened the window, studying the balcony and the narrow shelf that ran alongside it. Cautiously, he stepped out onto the narrow ledge, edging his way along the building's north side. He leaned his weight against the wall, going foot over foot, one step at a time. He paced his breathing so that it coincided with his gait. Step, breath, step, breath, until he could reach out to grab the iron railing of the next terrace. He took hold of it, then climbed over. The next few yards would be a snap, he thought, pausing to listen for sounds from the room. Nothing. He strode across the balcony, startled to feel the give in the bolts that riveted it to the building. The platform leaned at a twenty-degree angle with his weight as he stepped from it onto the ledge once more. He took a deep breath, then began the short half-steps that made every yard of distance seem like a mile.

Carter moved slowly but efficiently, careful not to get overconfident. To rouse a sleeping guest would result in his being arrested or shot outright. He kept reminding himself of this as if to tame an overwhelming impulse to hurry along recklessly. He hugged the side of the building, palms pressed against it as he crept nearer and nearer to the next balcony. He stood back, straight and tense, sidling the wall. Below him and across the street stood a small restaurant, two storefronts, and a movie theater. *Thank God there's no one down there*, he thought, taking note of his exposed position. The second balcony was within reach. He stopped and was about to take hold of the railing, when he heard the tapping sound of high heels on the pavement below. *Damn!* he cursed, freezing in his tracks. His breathing stopped. The sound of his pounding heart seemed audible as he glanced downward and caught a glimpse of a South African soldier and a prostitute.

"Where have you been?" the man asked drunkenly.

"You think you own me?" she shot back. "You ain't the only man in Johannesburg, you know."

The soldier must have grabbed her, because Carter could hear her grunt as he spoke in a throaty whisper.

"Look! See what I brought you? You like this, don't you?"

"Where did you get that?"

"That is for me to know, but if you want the cocaine, it comes with a price."

Carter listened, mesmerized, as she broke away from the soldier's grip.

"You are a pig!" she hissed.

"But you love me, don't you?"

There was a lull in their conversation as she considered his offer.

The next sound Carter heard was that of high heels tapping on the pavement once more. The soldier laughed. His stumbling footsteps sounded behind hers as they entered the Culembory Hotel together.

Carter closed his eyes solemnly. He ran his hand through his hair. It was wet with perspiration. He extended his arm tentatively, as much a feeler as an appendage, then grabbed the iron rail of the second balcony. He leaned over it, listening for sounds from inside the room before him. He peered inside, barely able to distinguish the silhouette of a figure in bed as it turned over, snoring. Carter leaped onto the balcony. He hurried across it, mounted the ledge, then stopped. Ten steps away stood the terrace leading to his own room.

Carter took Wilhelmina from her holster and attached a silencer. Any hesitancy that might have tempered his actions earlier had long since disappeared as he took the few remaining steps that separated him from his quarry. He was all professional now, and trained instinct—not prudence—was his master. Since Soviet hit men usually worked in teams of two, the odds of taking them both alive were slim. Even with the drop on them, Carter was pretty sure one or the other would fire. Still, he would attempt to keep this as clean as possible. These men would be valuable, if only for their general knowledge concerning KGB operations on the continent. Carter's expression grew taut as he came upon the edge of the balcony leading to his darkened room.

He stood stock-still. Not a sound emanated from within the room. Carter reached for the iron railing. It felt cold and forbidding. He eased himself over the top by degrees. His body tensed as he placed one foot on the terrace, shifting his weight from the ledge. A tingling sensation of panic cut through him in an instant. The balcony was breaking away from its moorings!

Carter's eyes shot to the window as he stood half on and

half off the ledge. He prayed that the men inside hadn't heard
him and that the balcony would support him for the few
seconds it would take to get off three or four rounds. His
temples ached, the blood in his head throbbing. His eyes
lifted to the window again. If the Soviets had heard anything,
they hadn't reacted. Yet.

He steeled his jangled nerves. Inch by inch, pound by
pound, he lowered himself onto the balcony. Below him he
could hear the sound of plaster and cement as it sprinkled
down to the pavement. He visualized the room's layout
before making his move: a desk, a bureau with mirror, and a
bed that hugged the north wall. *Now!* his mind said. He threw
his full weight down onto the balcony. He fired. One, two,
three shots crashed through the window. He heard the cry of a
man. It was the last sound he heard before tumbling down to
the deadly whistle of return fire. Carter had no time to react as
he plunged the ten feet to the floor below. Wilhelmina,
frozen in his right hand, fired randomly as he slammed,
shoulder first, onto the floor of the terrace. He looked up.
Above him, the third-floor balcony dangled precariously
from its one remaining support.

—From THE BLUE ICE AFFAIR
A New Nick Carter Spy Thriller
From Charter in February 1985

☐ 74965-8	**SAN JUAN INFERNO**	$2.50
☐ 71539-7	**RETREAT FOR DEATH**	$2.50
☐ 79073-9	**THE STRONTIUM CODE**	$2.50
☐ 79077-1	**THE SUICIDE SEAT**	$2.25
☐ 82726-8	**TURKISH BLOODBATH**	$2.25
☐ 09157-1	**CARIBBEAN COUP**	$2.50
☐ 14220-6	**DEATH ISLAND**	$2.50
☐ 95935-0	**ZERO-HOUR STRIKE FORCE**	$2.50
☐ 03223-0	**ASSIGNMENT: RIO**	$2.50
☐ 13918-3	**DAY OF THE MAHDI**	$2.50
☐ 14222-2	**DEATH HAND PLAY**	$2.50
☐ 29782-X	**THE GOLDEN BULL**	$2.50
☐ 45520-4	**THE KREMLIN KILL**	$2.50
☐ 52276-9	**THE MAYAN CONNECTION**	$2.50

Prices may be slightly higher in Canada.

A8